SECRET CODERS
Paths & Portals

GENE LUEN YANG
& MIKE HOLMES

:01
First Second
New York

"It was this wonderful time between magic and so-called rationality."

–Wally Feurzeig, co-creator of the Logo programming language, on the early days of Logo

First Second

New York

Copyright © 2016 by Humble Comics LLC

Published by First Second
First Second is an imprint of Roaring Brook Press,
a division of Holtzbrinck Publishing Holdings Limited Partnership
175 Fifth Avenue, New York, NY 10010

Cataloging-in-Publication Data is on file at the Library of Congress

Paperback ISBN: 978-1-62672-076-3
Hardcover ISBN: 978-1-62672-340-5

Our books may be purchased in bulk for promotional, educational,
or business use. Please contact your local bookseller or the Macmillan
Corporate and Premium Sales Department at (800) 221-7945 x5442
or by email at MacmillanSpecialMarkets@macmillan.com.

First edition 2016

Book design by Rob Steen

Printed in China by Toppan Leefung Printing Ltd., Dongguan City, Guangdong Province

Paperback: 10 9 8 7 6
Hardcover: 10 9 8 7 6 5 4 3 2 1

Chapter

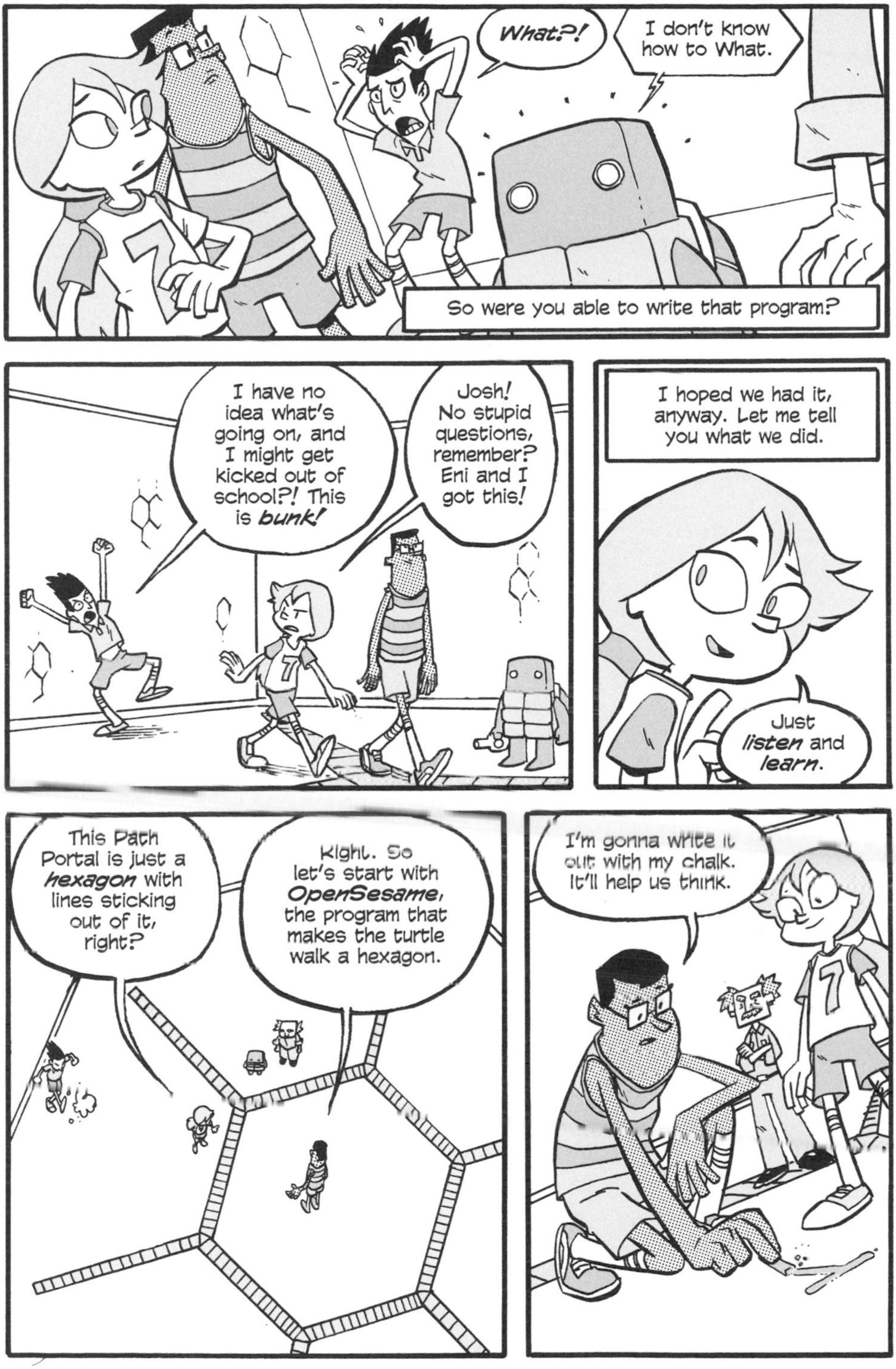
What?!
I don't know how to What.
So were you able to write that program?
I have no idea what's going on, and I might get kicked out of school?! This is *bunk!*
Josh! No stupid questions, remember? Eni and I got this!
I hoped we had it, anyway. Let me tell you what we did.
Just *listen* and *learn*.
This Path Portal is just a *hexagon* with lines sticking out of it, right?
Right. So let's start with *OpenSesame*, the program that makes the turtle walk a hexagon.
I'm gonna write it out with my chalk. It'll help us think.

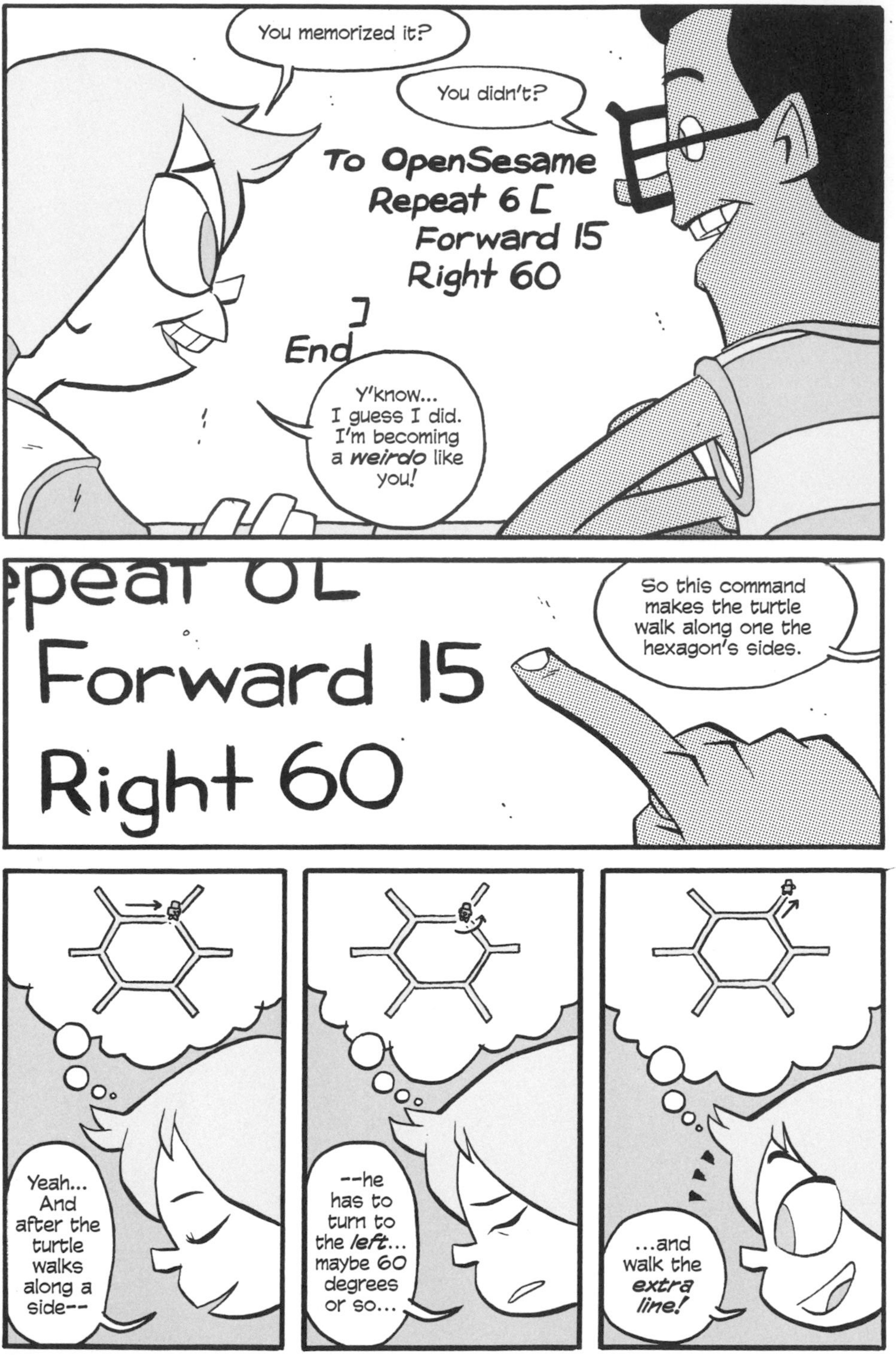

You memorized it?
You didn't?
To OpenSesame
Repeat 6 [
Forward 15
Right 60
]
End
Y'know... I guess I did. I'm becoming a *weirdo* like you!
epeat 6[
Forward 15
Right 60
So this command makes the turtle walk along one the hexagon's sides.
Yeah... And after the turtle walks along a side--
--he has to turn to the *left*... maybe 60 degrees or so...
...and walk the ***extra line!***

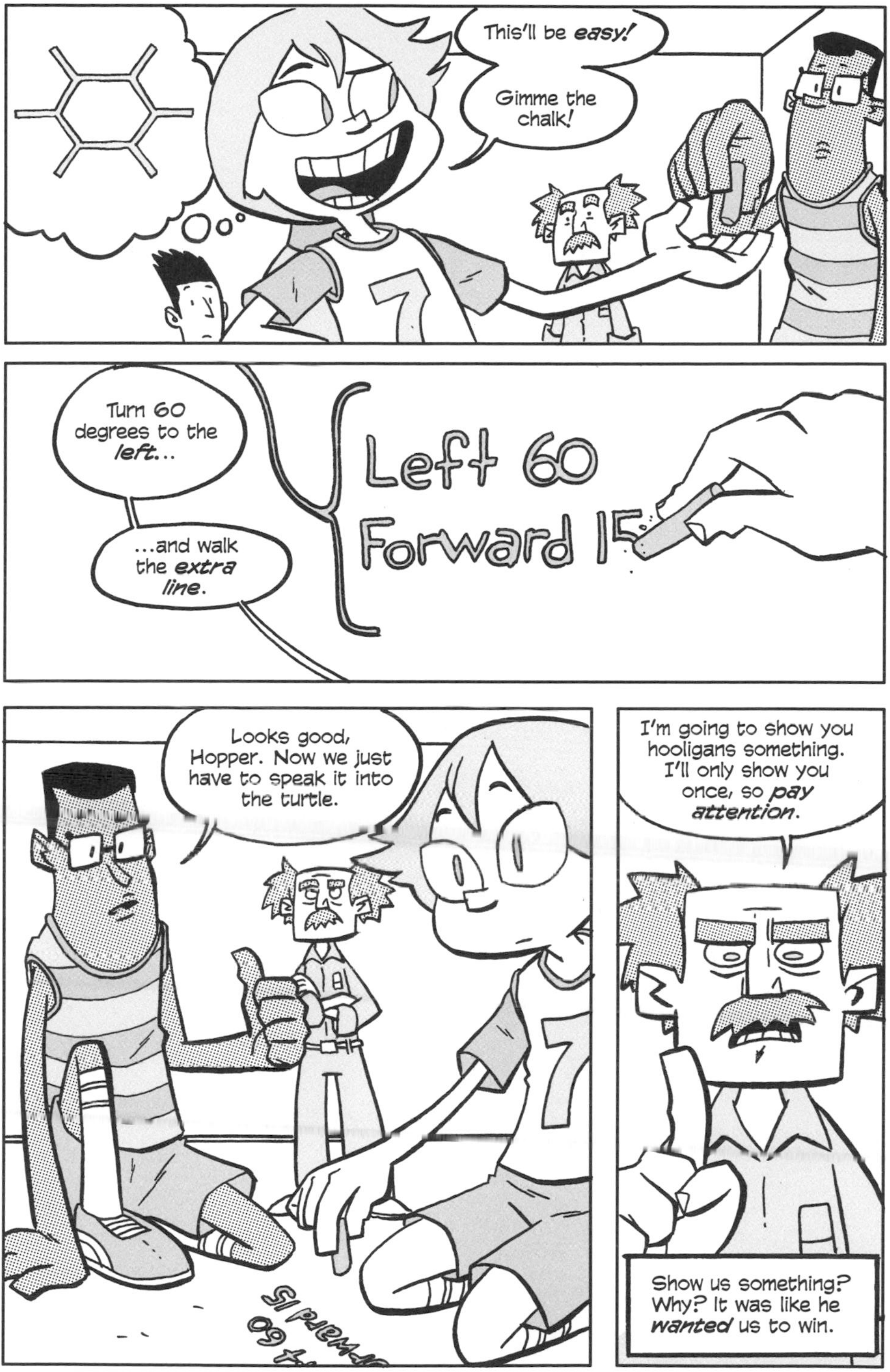
This'll be *easy!*
Gimme the chalk!
Turn 60 degrees to the *left*...
...and walk the *extra line*.
Left 60
Forward 15
Looks good, Hopper. Now we just have to speak it into the turtle.
I'm going to show you hooligans something. I'll only show you once, so *pay attention*.
Show us something? Why? It was like he *wanted* us to win.

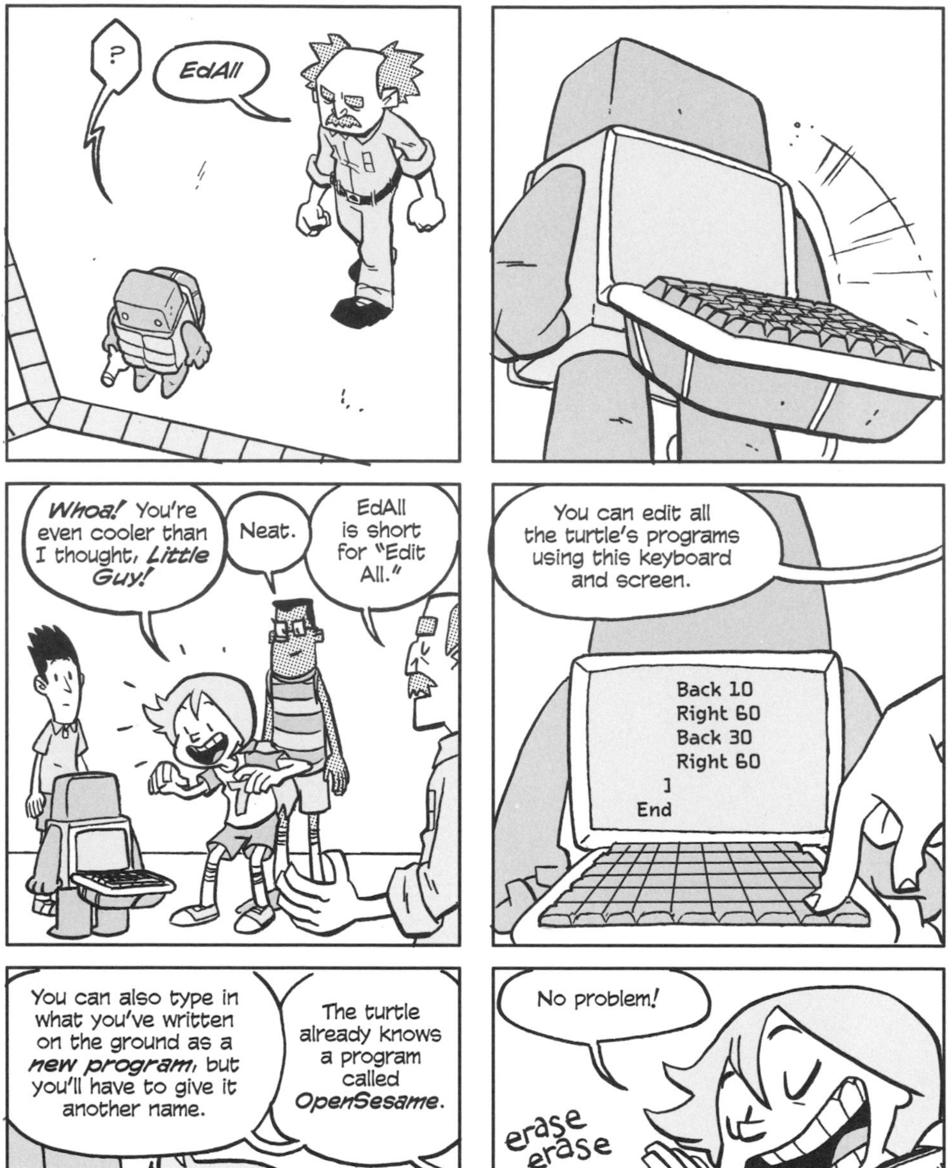
?
EdAll
Whoa! You're even cooler than I thought, Little Guy!
Neat.
EdAll is short for "Edit All."
You can edit all the turtle's programs using this keyboard and screen.
Back 10
Right 60
Back 30
Right 60
]
End
You can also type in what you've written on the ground as a new program, but you'll have to give it another name.
The turtle already knows a program called OpenSesame.
No problem!
erase erase
forward
right 60

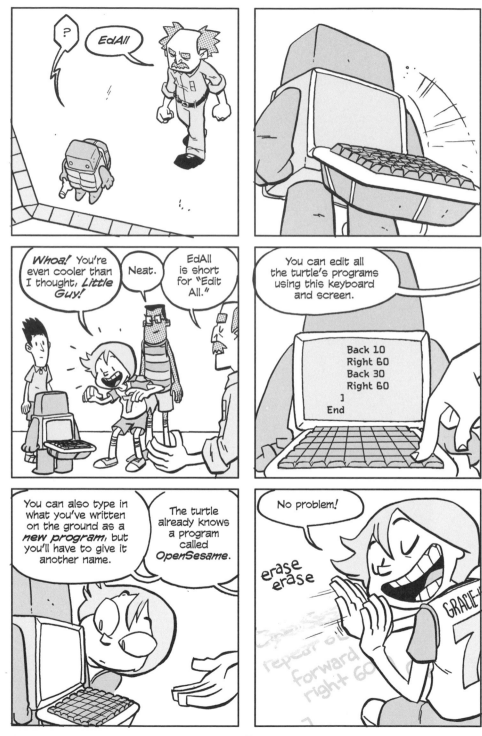

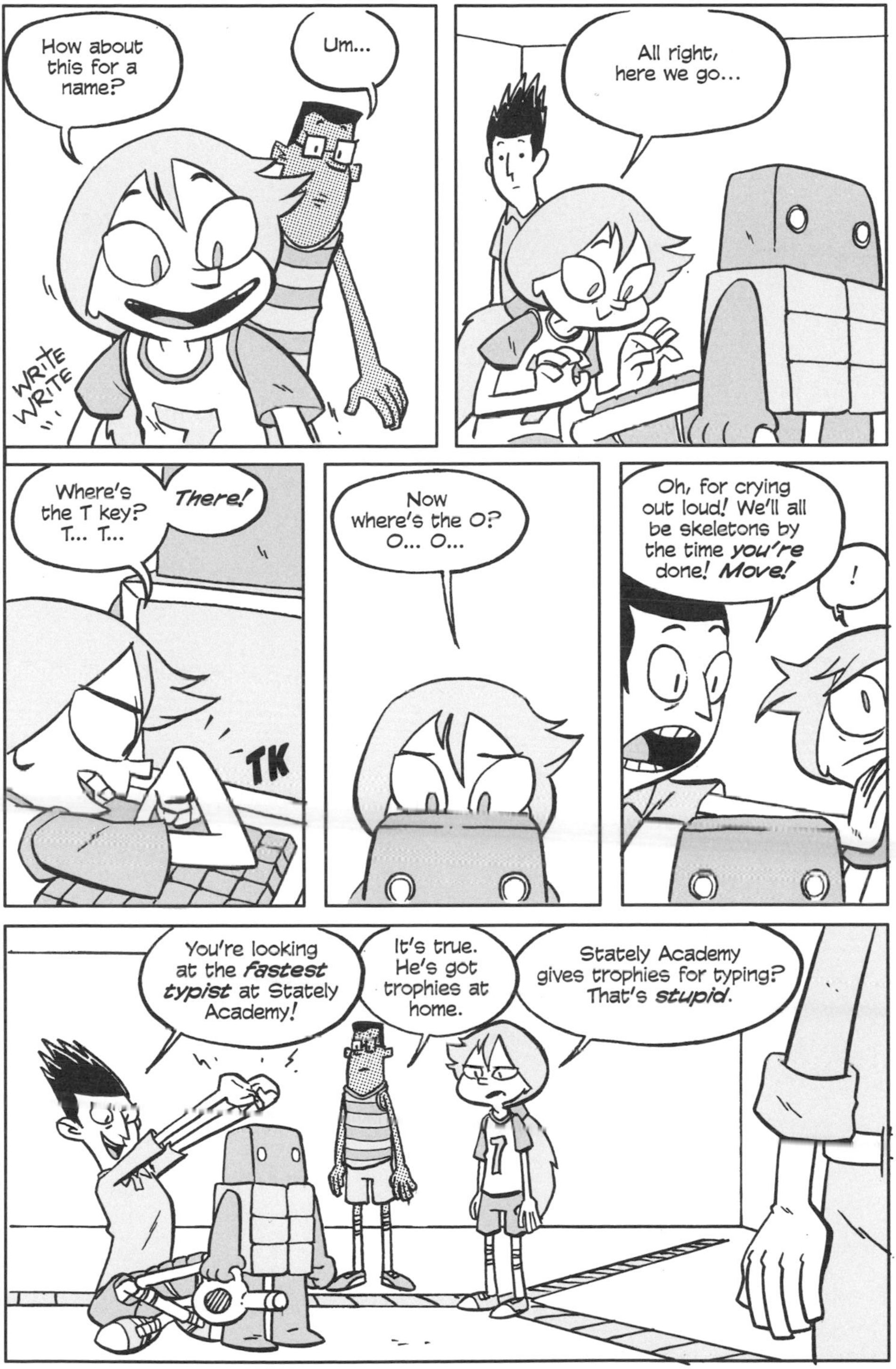
How about this for a name?
Um...
WRITE WRITE
All right, here we go...
Where's the T key? T... T...
There!
TK
Now where's the O? O... O...
Oh, for crying out loud! We'll all be skeletons by the time *you're* done! *Move!*
!
You're looking at the *fastest typist* at Stately Academy!
It's true. He's got trophies at home.
Stately Academy gives trophies for typing? That's *stupid*.

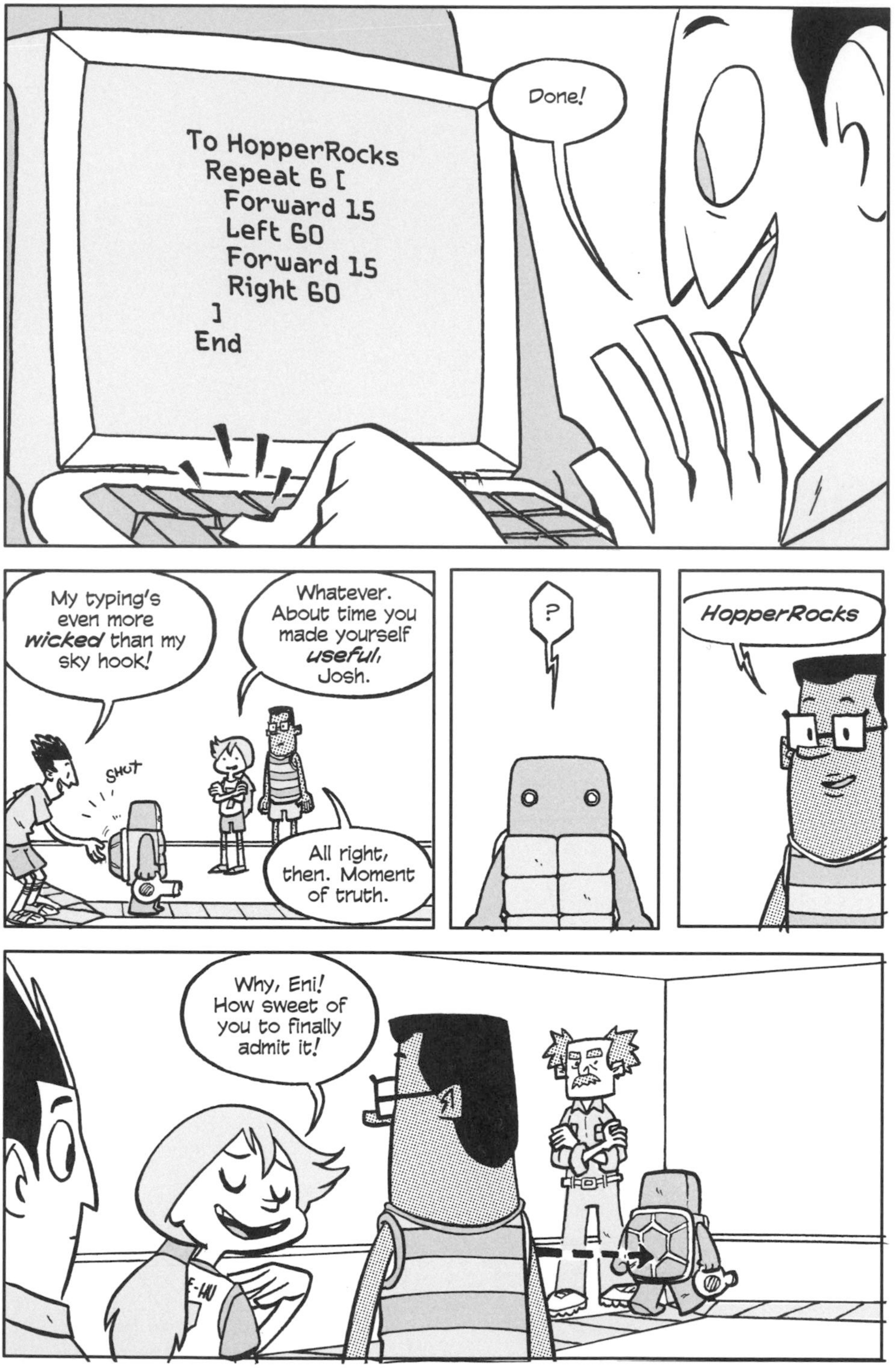

To HopperRocks
Repeat 6 [
Forward 15
Left 60
Forward 15
Right 60
]
End
Done!
My typing's even more *wicked* than my sky hook!
SHUT
Whatever. About time you made yourself *useful*, Josh.
All right, then. Moment of truth.
?
HopperRocks
Why, Eni! How sweet of you to finally admit it!

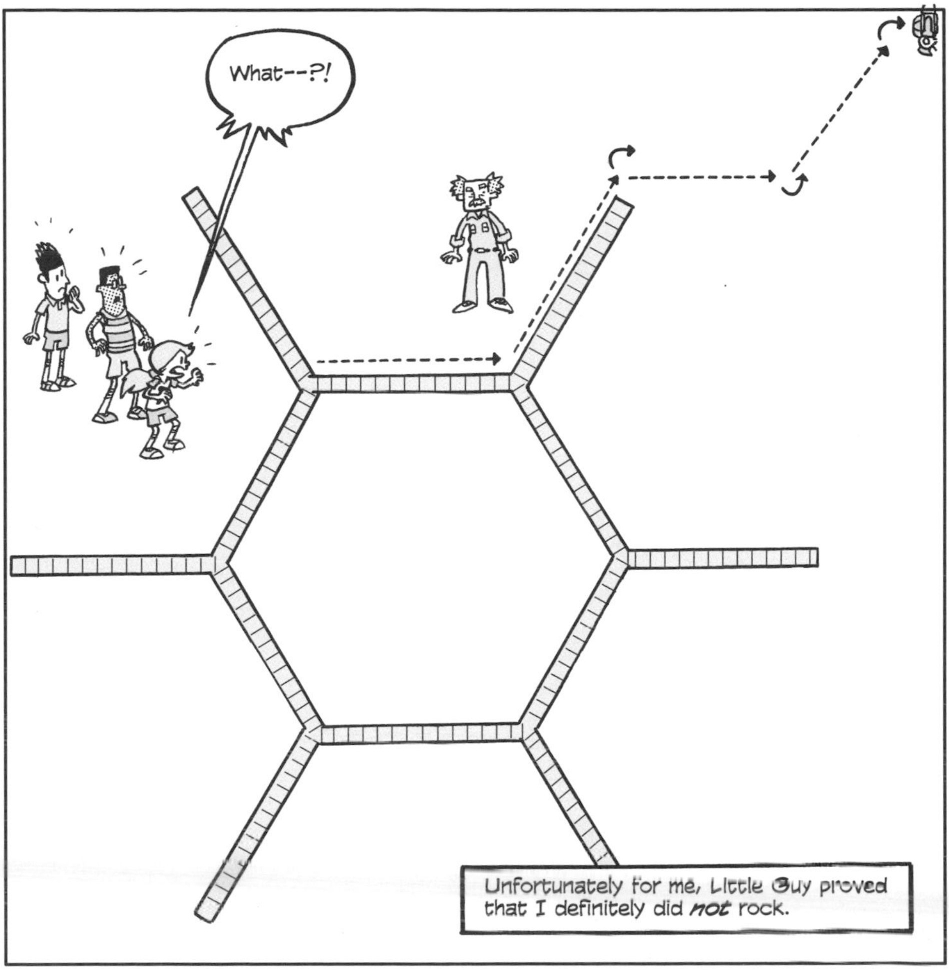
What--?!
Unfortunately for me, Little Guy proved that I definitely did *not* rock.

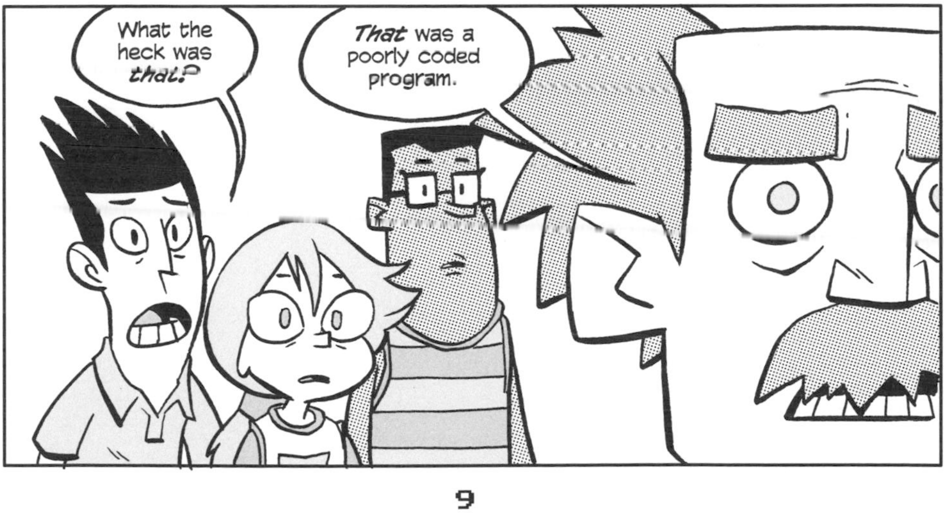
What the heck was *that*?
That was a poorly coded program.

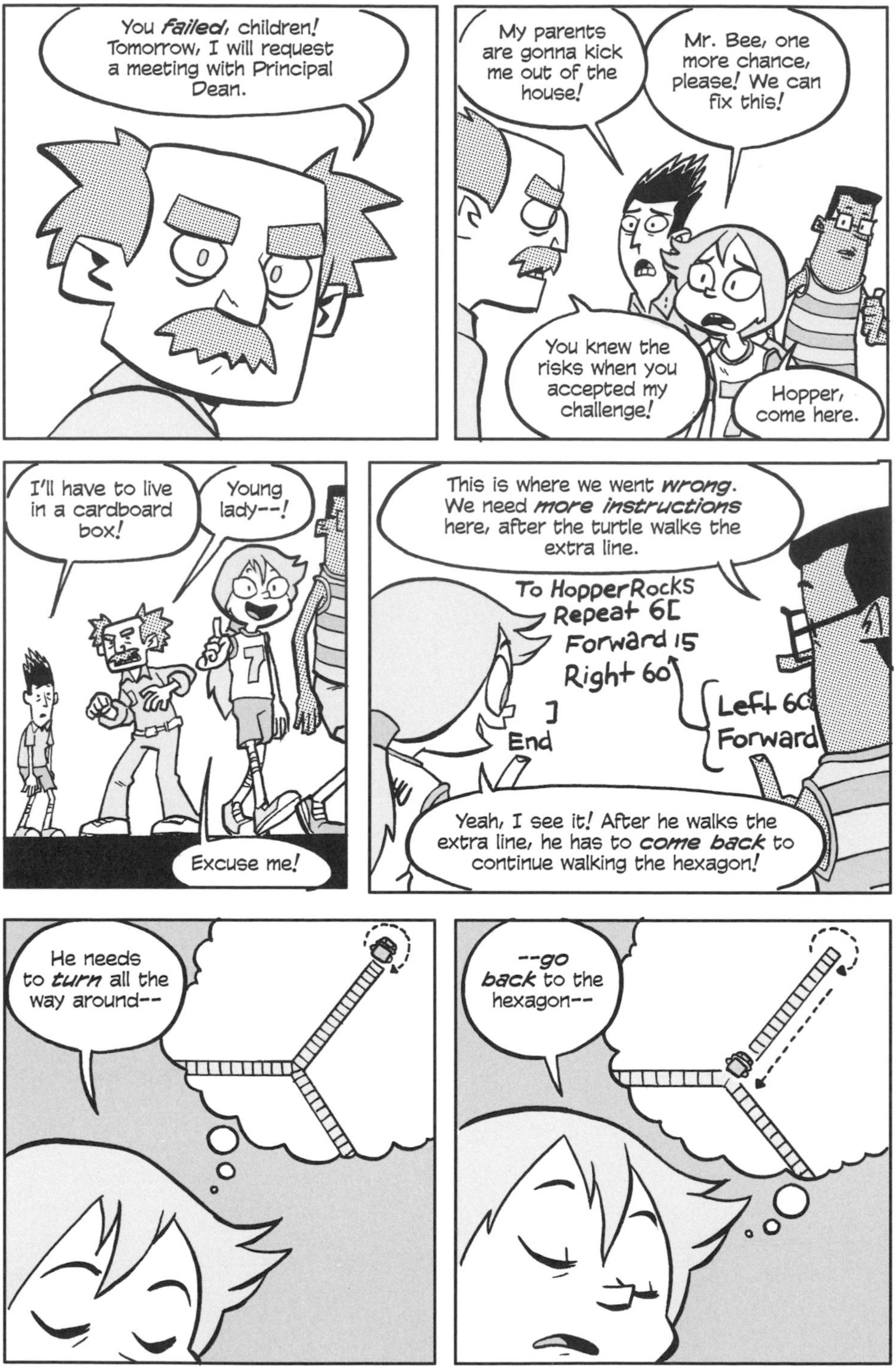
You *failed*, children! Tomorrow, I will request a meeting with Principal Dean.
My parents are gonna kick me out of the house!
Mr. Bee, one more chance, please! We can fix this!
You knew the risks when you accepted my challenge!
Hopper, come here.
I'll have to live in a cardboard box!
Young lady--!
Excuse me!
This is where we went *wrong*. We need *more instructions* here, after the turtle walks the extra line.
To HopperRocks
Repeat 6[
Forward 15
Right 60
]
End
Left 60
Forward
Yeah, I see it! After he walks the extra line, he has to *come back* to continue walking the hexagon!
He needs to *turn* all the way around--
--*go back* to the hexagon--

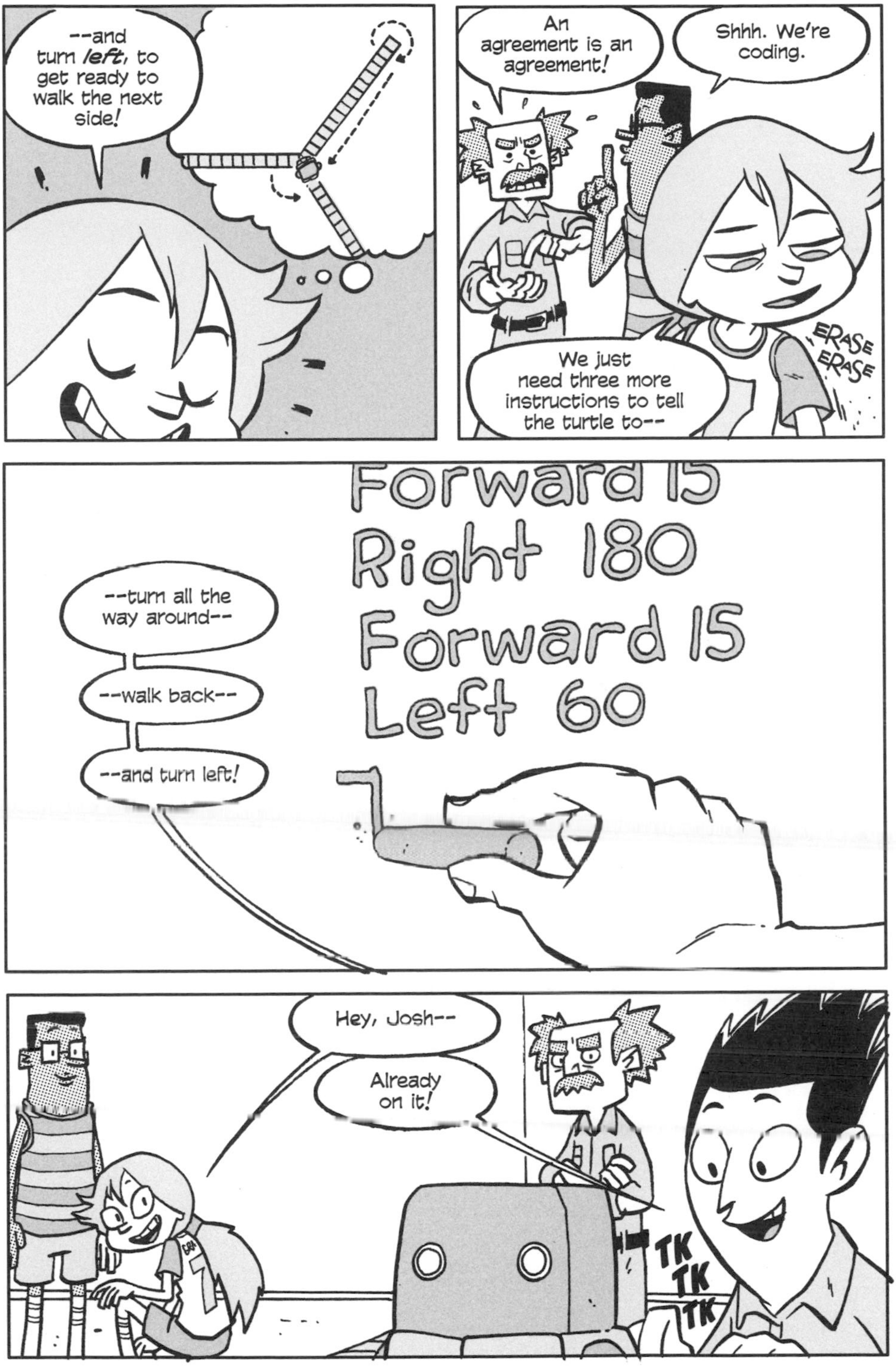
--and turn *left*, to get ready to walk the next side!
An agreement is an agreement!
Shhh. We're coding.
We just need three more instructions to tell the turtle to--
ERASE ERASE
Forward 15
Right 180
Forward 15
Left 60
--turn all the way around--
--walk back--
--and turn left!
Hey, Josh--
Already on it!
TK TK TK

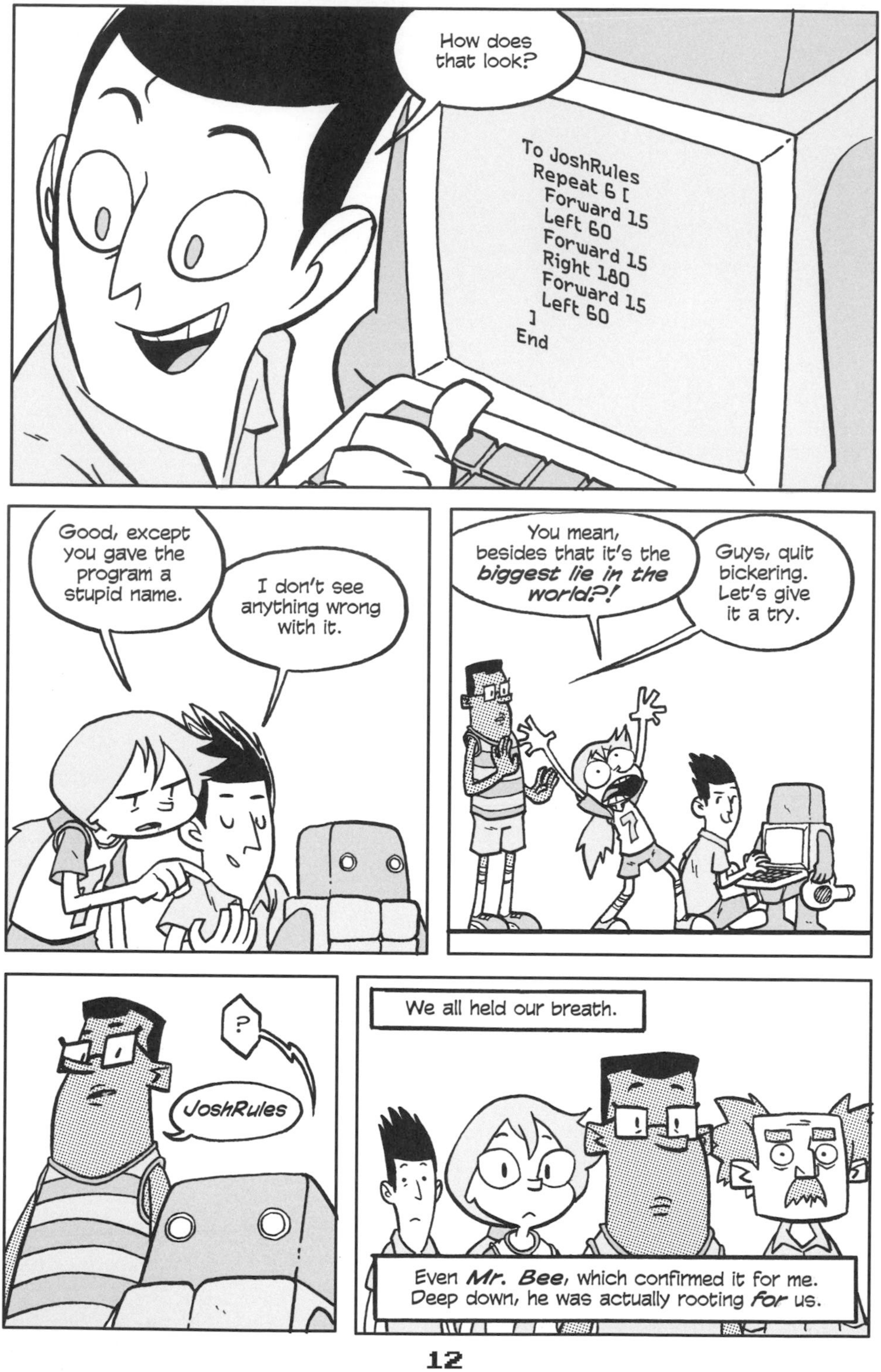
How does that look?
To JoshRules
Repeat 6 [
Forward 15
Left 60
Forward 15
Right 180
Forward 15
Left 60
]
End
Good, except you gave the program a stupid name.
I don't see anything wrong with it.
You mean, besides that it's the *biggest lie in the world?!*
Guys, quit bickering. Let's give it a try.
JoshRules
?
We all held our breath.
Even ***Mr. Bee***, which confirmed it for me. Deep down, he was actually rooting ***for*** us.

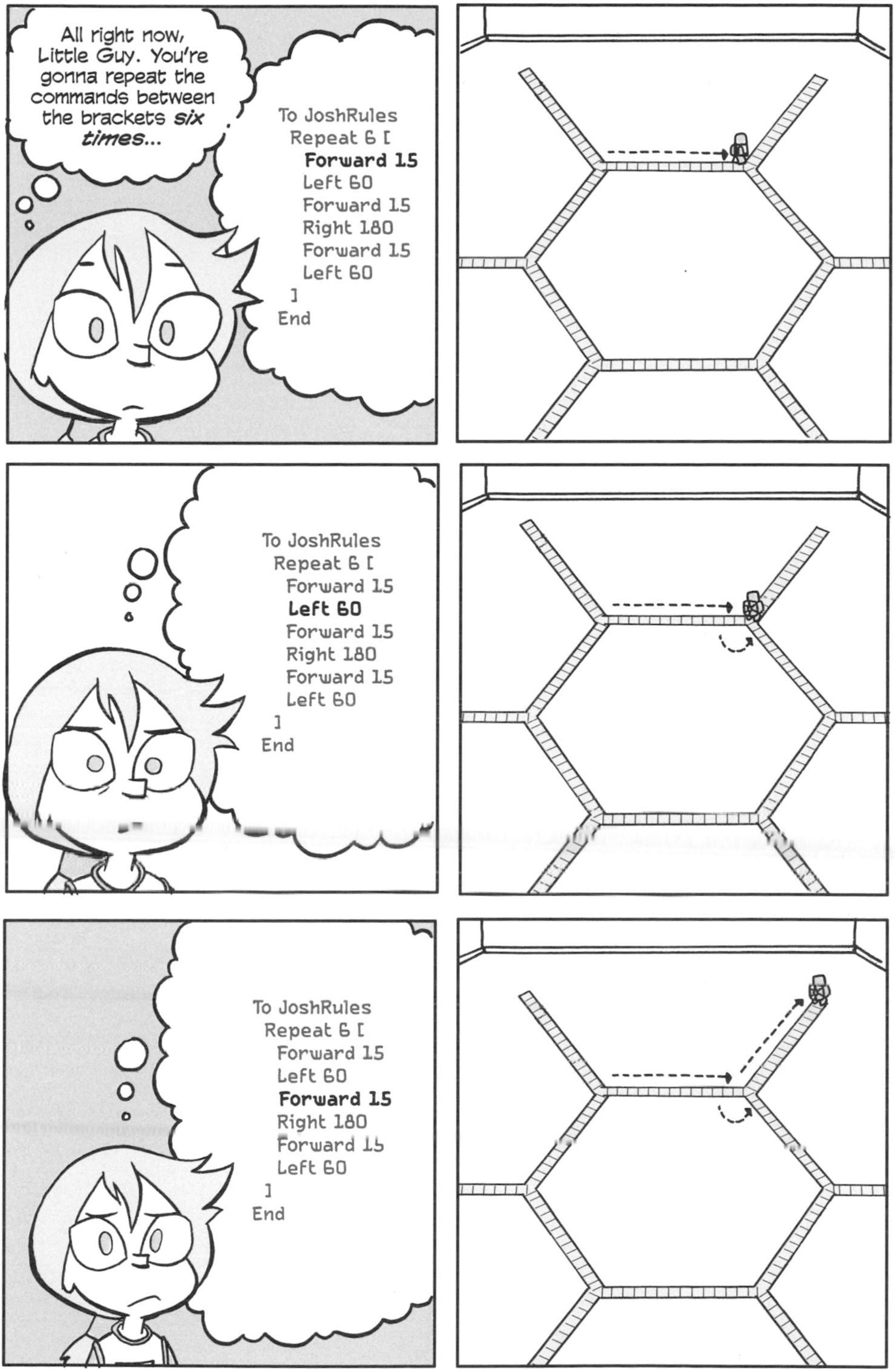
All right now, Little Guy. You're gonna repeat the commands between the brackets *six times*...
To JoshRules
Repeat 6 [
Forward 15
Left 60
Forward 15
Right 180
Forward 15
Left 60
]
End
To JoshRules
Repeat 6 [
Forward 15
Left 60
Forward 15
Right 180
Forward 15
Left 60
]
End
To JoshRules
Repeat 6 [
Forward 15
Left 60
Forward 15
Right 180
Forward 15
Left 60
]
End

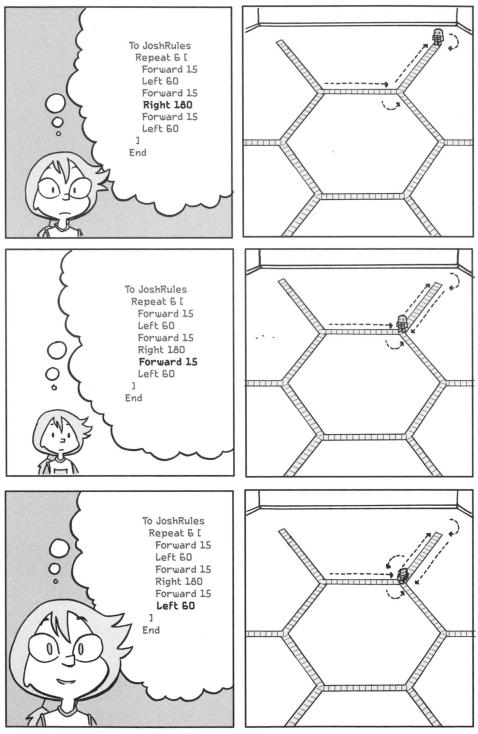

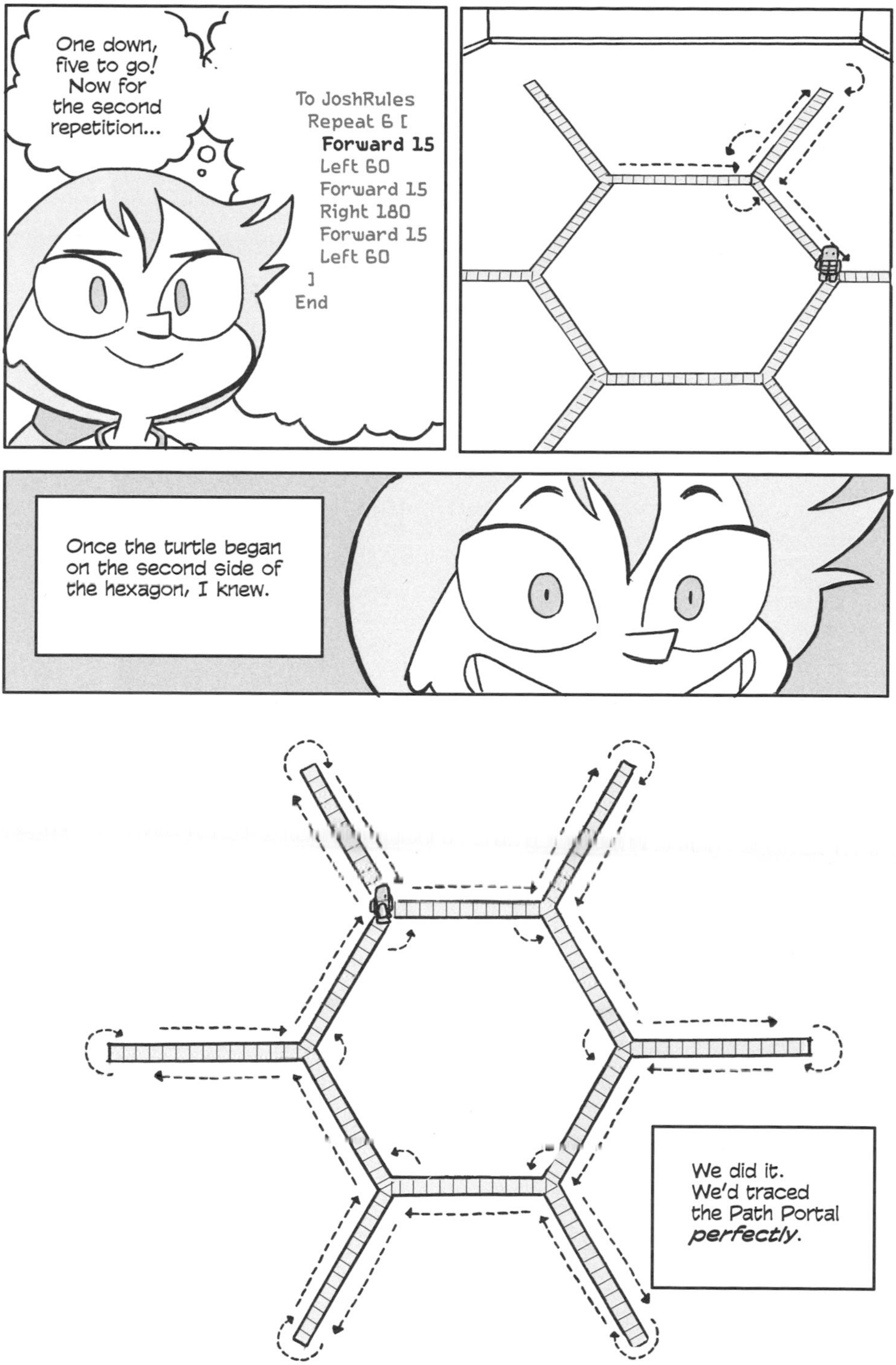

One down, five to go! Now for the second repetition...
To JoshRules
Repeat 6 [
Forward 15
Left 60
Forward 15
Right 180
Forward 15
Left 60
]
End
Once the turtle began on the second side of the hexagon, I knew.
We did it. We'd traced the Path Portal *perfectly*.

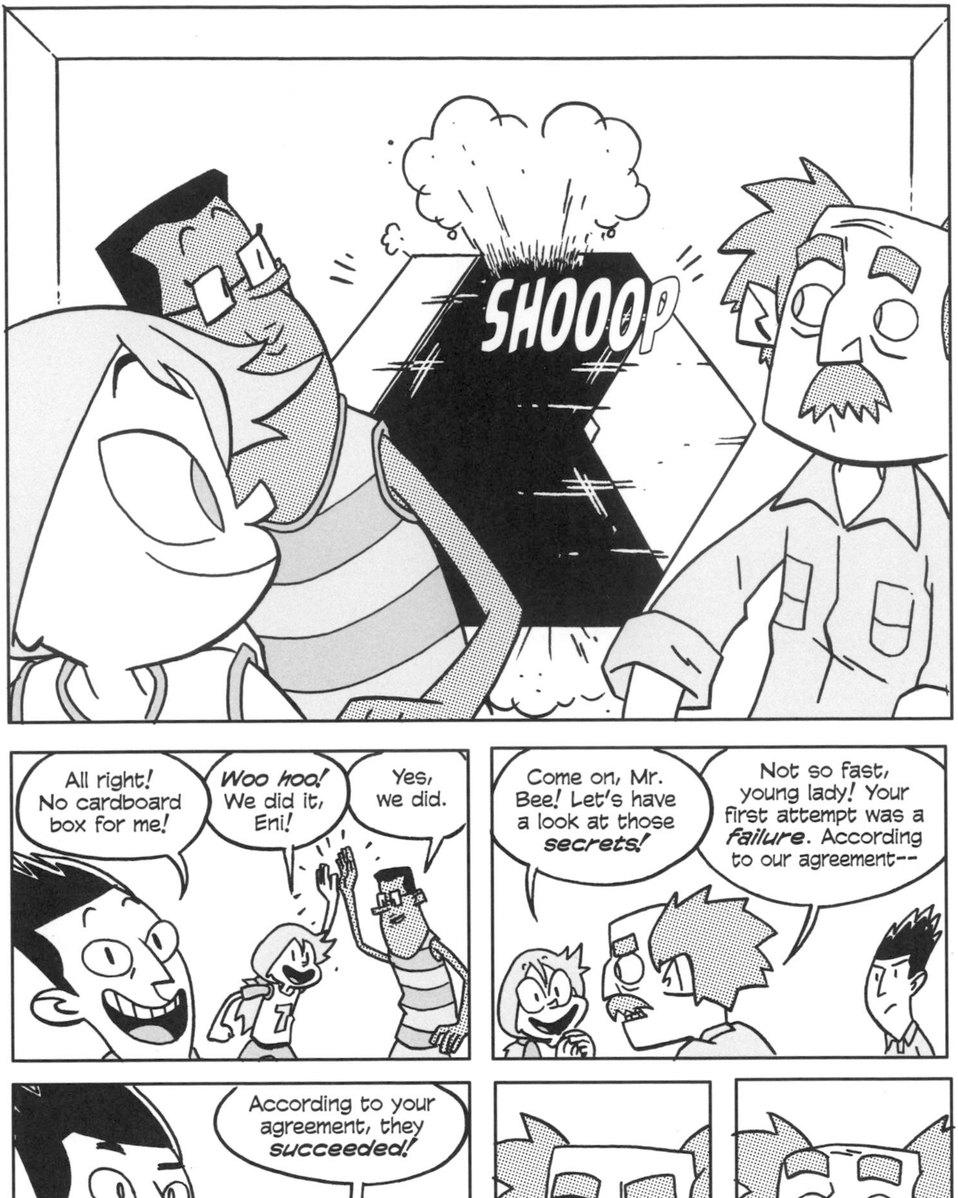

SHOOOP
All right! No cardboard box for me!
Woo hoo! We did it, Eni!
Yes, we did.
Come on, Mr. Bee! Let's have a look at those ***secrets!***
Not so fast, young lady! Your first attempt was a ***failure***. According to our agreement--
According to your agreement, they ***succeeded!***
You never said ***anything*** about the number of attempts they were allowed!

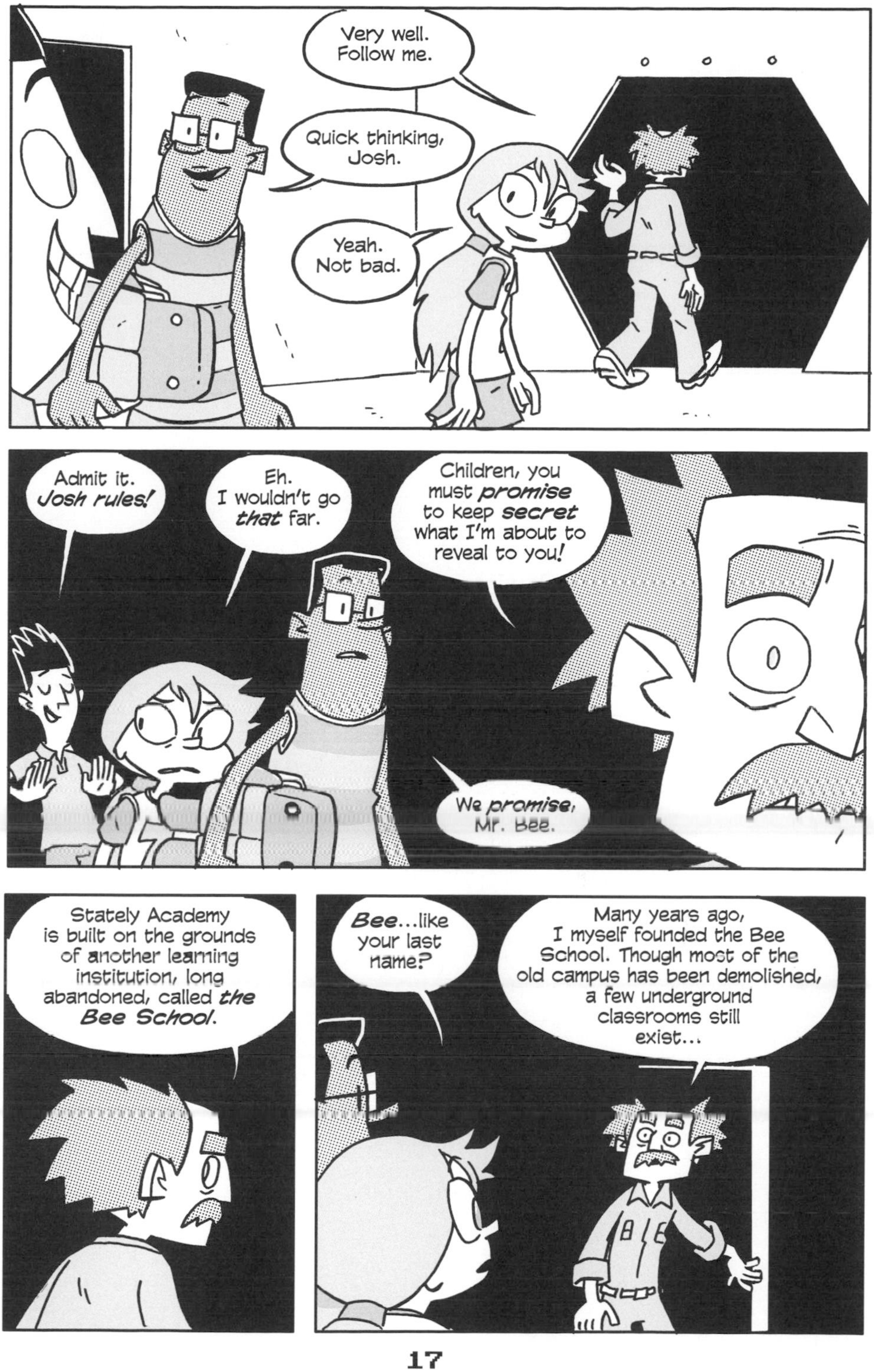
Very well. Follow me.
Quick thinking, Josh.
Yeah. Not bad.
Admit it. *Josh rules!*
Eh. I wouldn't go *that* far.
Children, you must *promise* to keep *secret* what I'm about to reveal to you!
We *promise*, Mr. Bee.
Stately Academy is built on the grounds of another learning institution, long abandoned, called *the Bee School*.
Bee...like your last name?
Many years ago, I myself founded the Bee School. Though most of the old campus has been demolished, a few underground classrooms still exist...

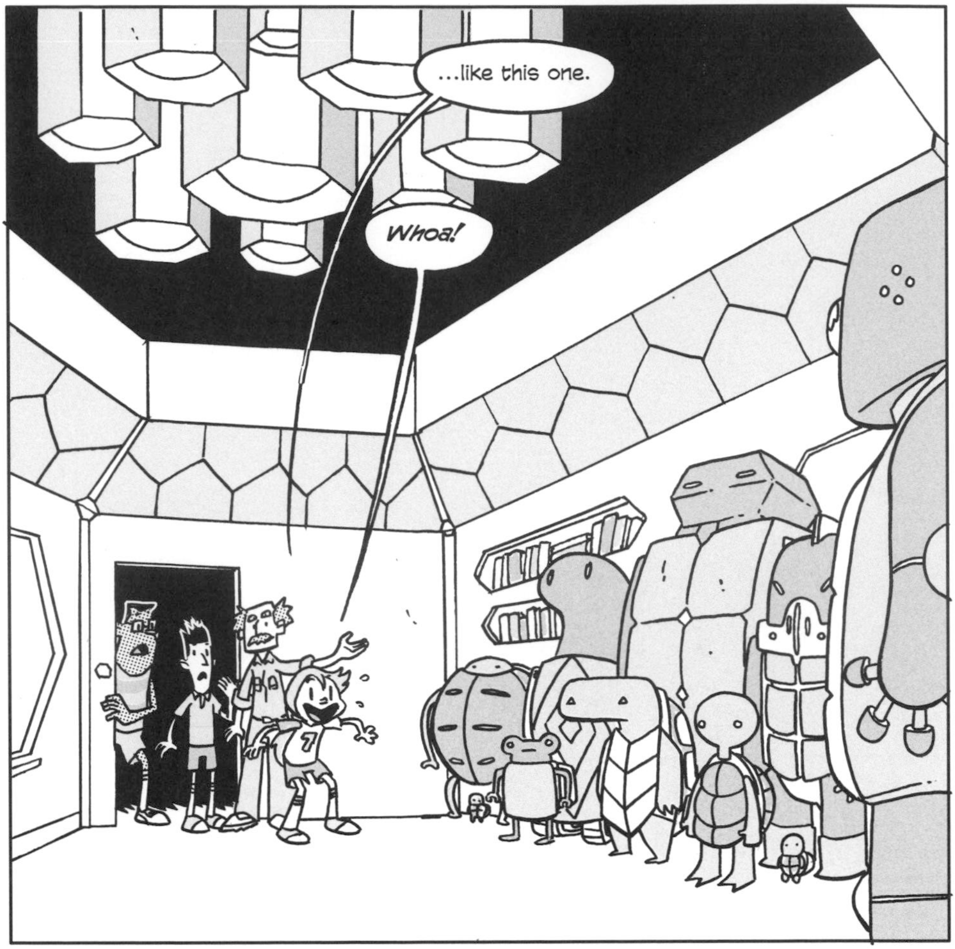
...like this one.
Whoa!

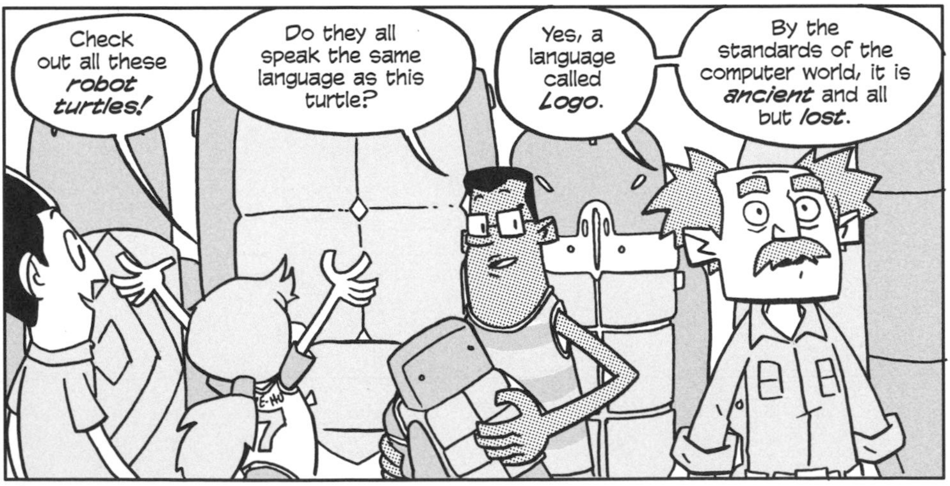
Check out all these *robot turtles!*
Do they all speak the same language as this turtle?
Yes, a language called *Logo*.
By the standards of the computer world, it is *ancient* and all but *lost*.

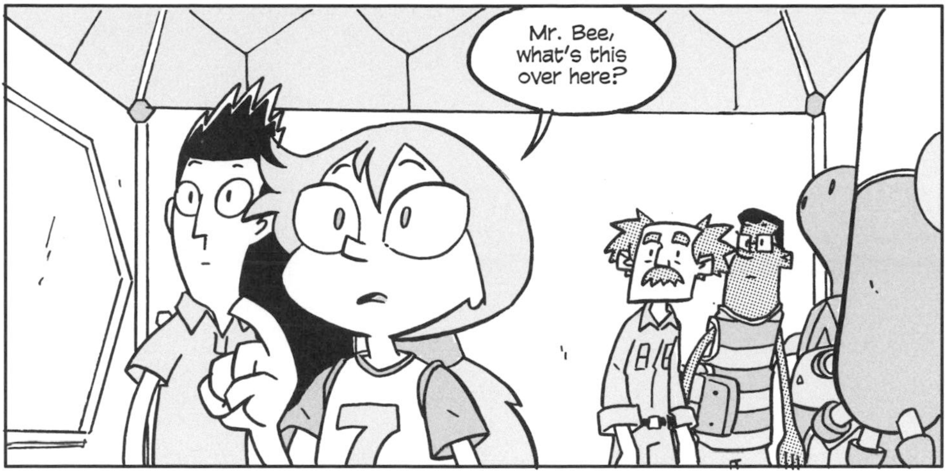
Mr. Bee, what's this over here?

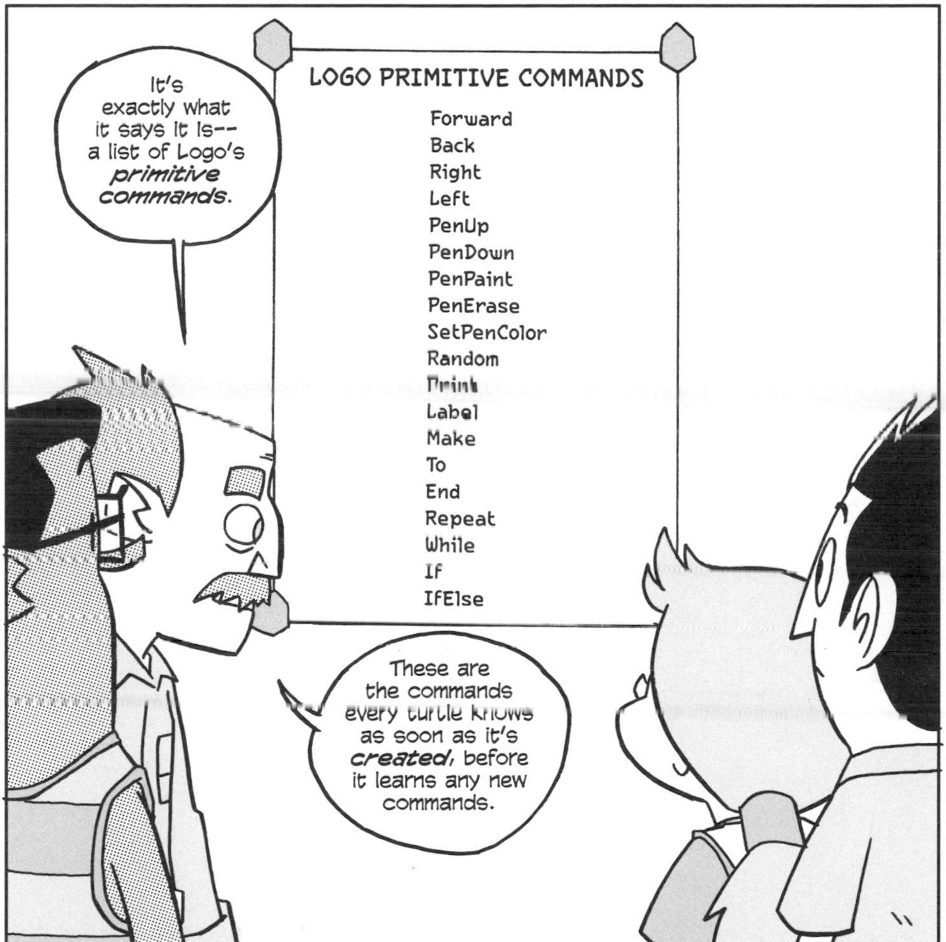
It's exactly what it says it is-- a list of Logo's *primitive commands*.
LOGO PRIMITIVE COMMANDS
Forward
Back
Right
Left
PenUp
PenDown
PenPaint
PenErase
SetPenColor
Random
Print
Label
Make
To
End
Repeat
While
If
IfElse
These are the commands every turtle knows as soon as it's *created*, before it learns any new commands.

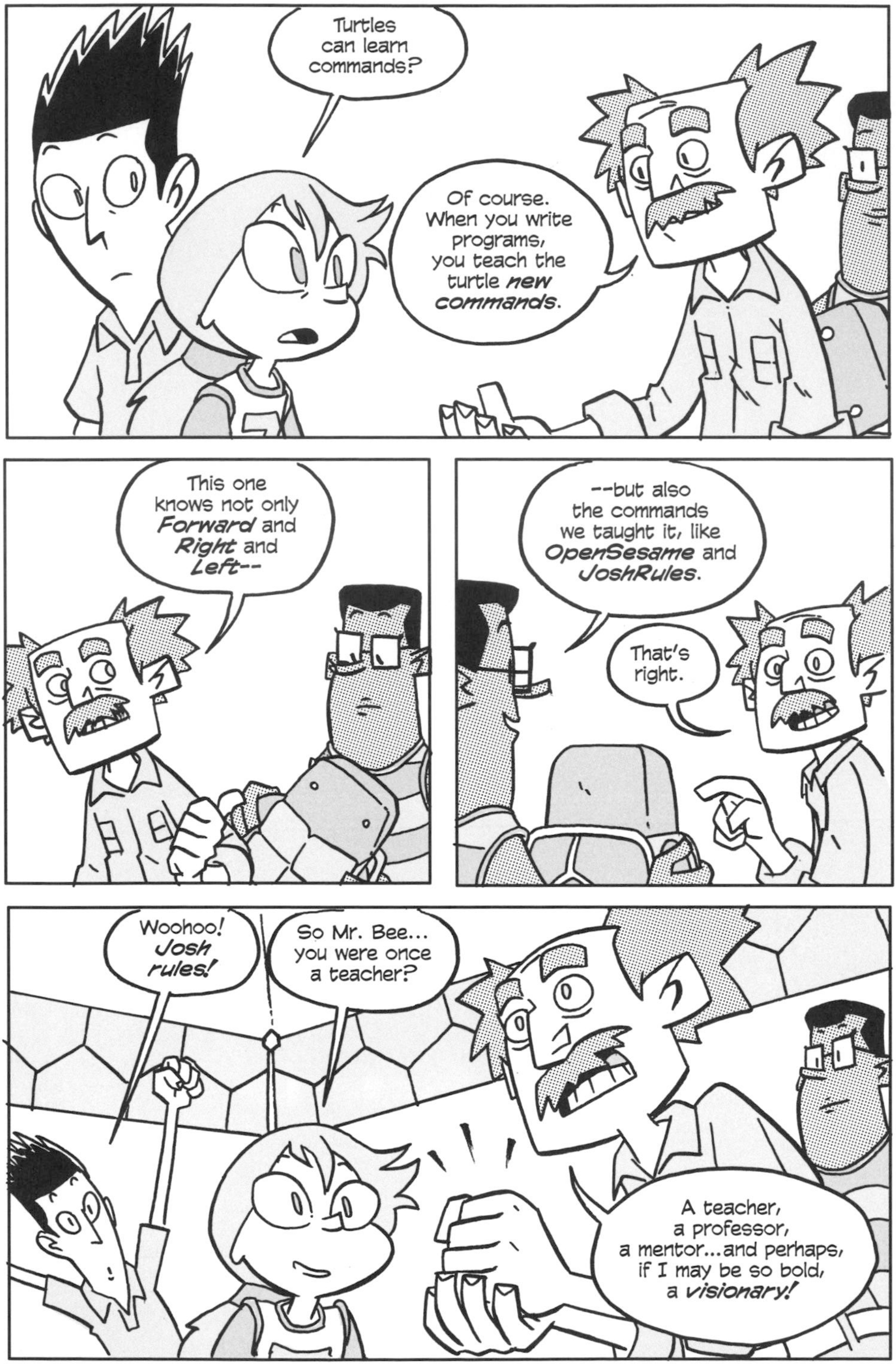

Turtles can learn commands?
Of course. When you write programs, you teach the turtle *new commands*.
This one knows not only *Forward* and *Right* and *Left*--
--but also the commands we taught it, like *OpenSesame* and *JoshRules*.
That's right.
Woohoo! *Josh rules!*
So Mr. Bee... you were once a teacher?
A teacher, a professor, a mentor...and perhaps, if I may be so bold, a *visionary!*

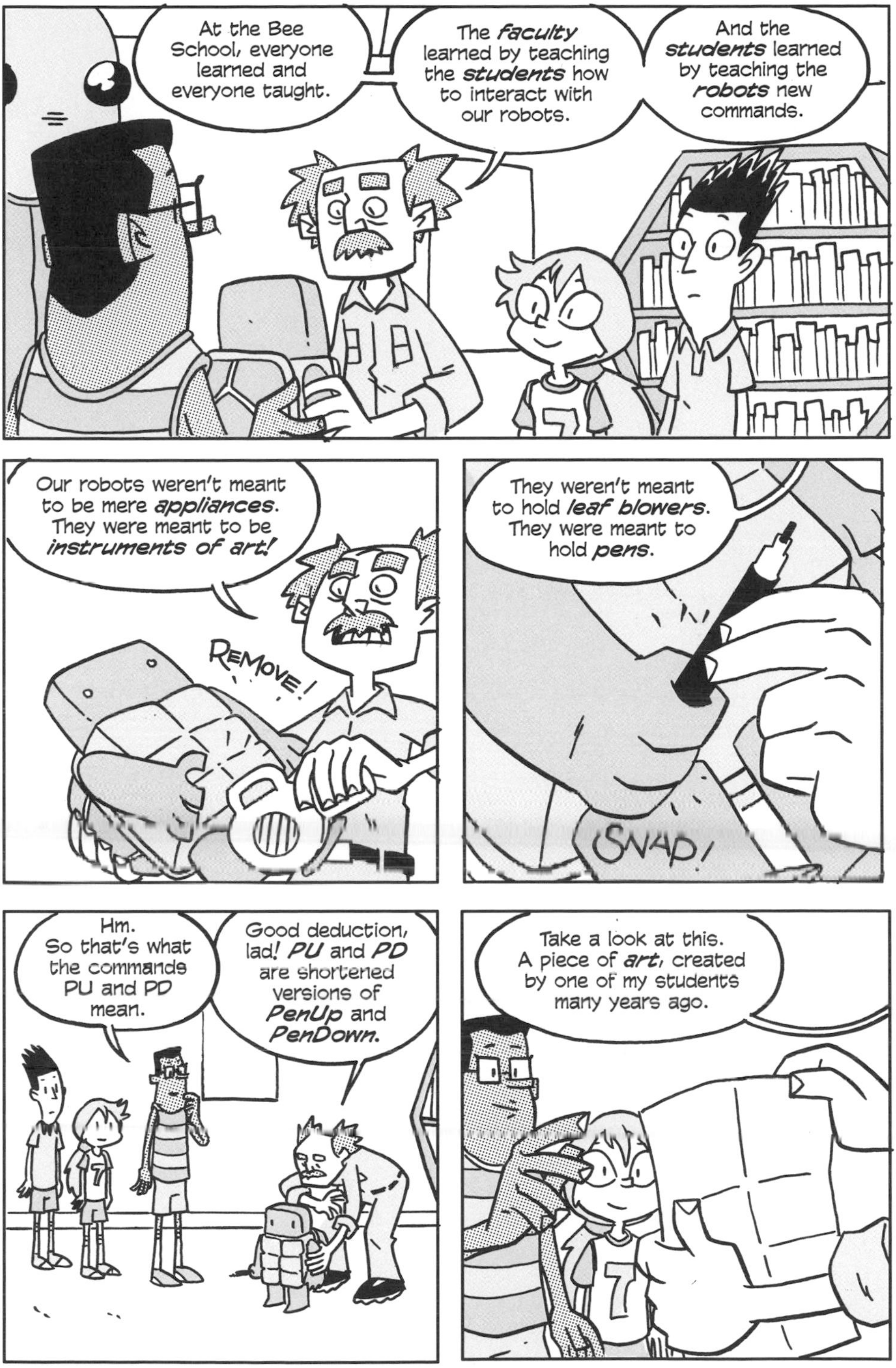

At the Bee School, everyone learned and everyone taught.
The *faculty* learned by teaching the *students* how to interact with our robots.
And the *students* learned by teaching the *robots* new commands.
Our robots weren't meant to be mere *appliances*. They were meant to be *instruments of art!*
REMOVE!
They weren't meant to hold *leaf blowers*. They were meant to hold *pens*.
SNAP!
Hm. So that's what the commands PU and PD mean.
Good deduction, lad! *PU* and *PD* are shortened versions of *PenUp* and *PenDown*.
Take a look at this. A piece of *art*, created by one of my students many years ago.

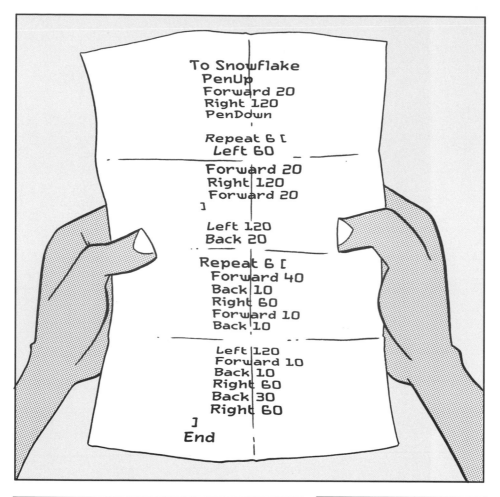

```
To Snowflake
PenUp
Forward 20
Right 120
PenDown

Repeat 6 [
    Left 60

Forward 20
Right 120
Forward 20
]

Left 120
Back 20

Repeat 6 [
    Forward 40
    Back 10
    Right 60
    Forward 10
    Back 10

Left 120
Forward 10
Back 10
Right 60
Back 30
Right 60
]
End
```

It's already keyed into this turtle. Go on. Give it a try.

?

Snowflake

Wicked!

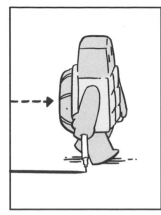

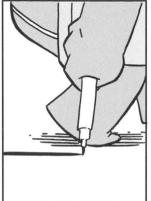

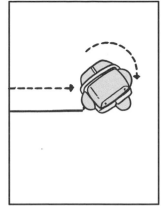

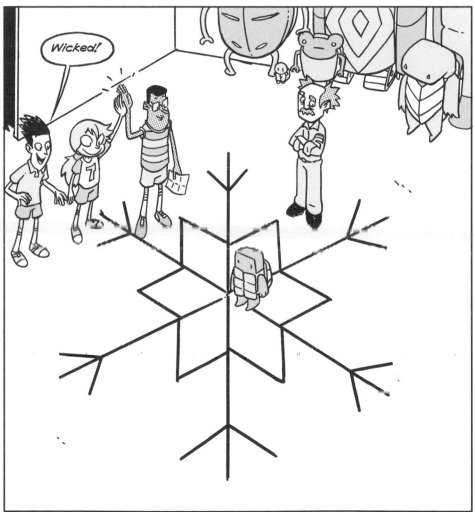

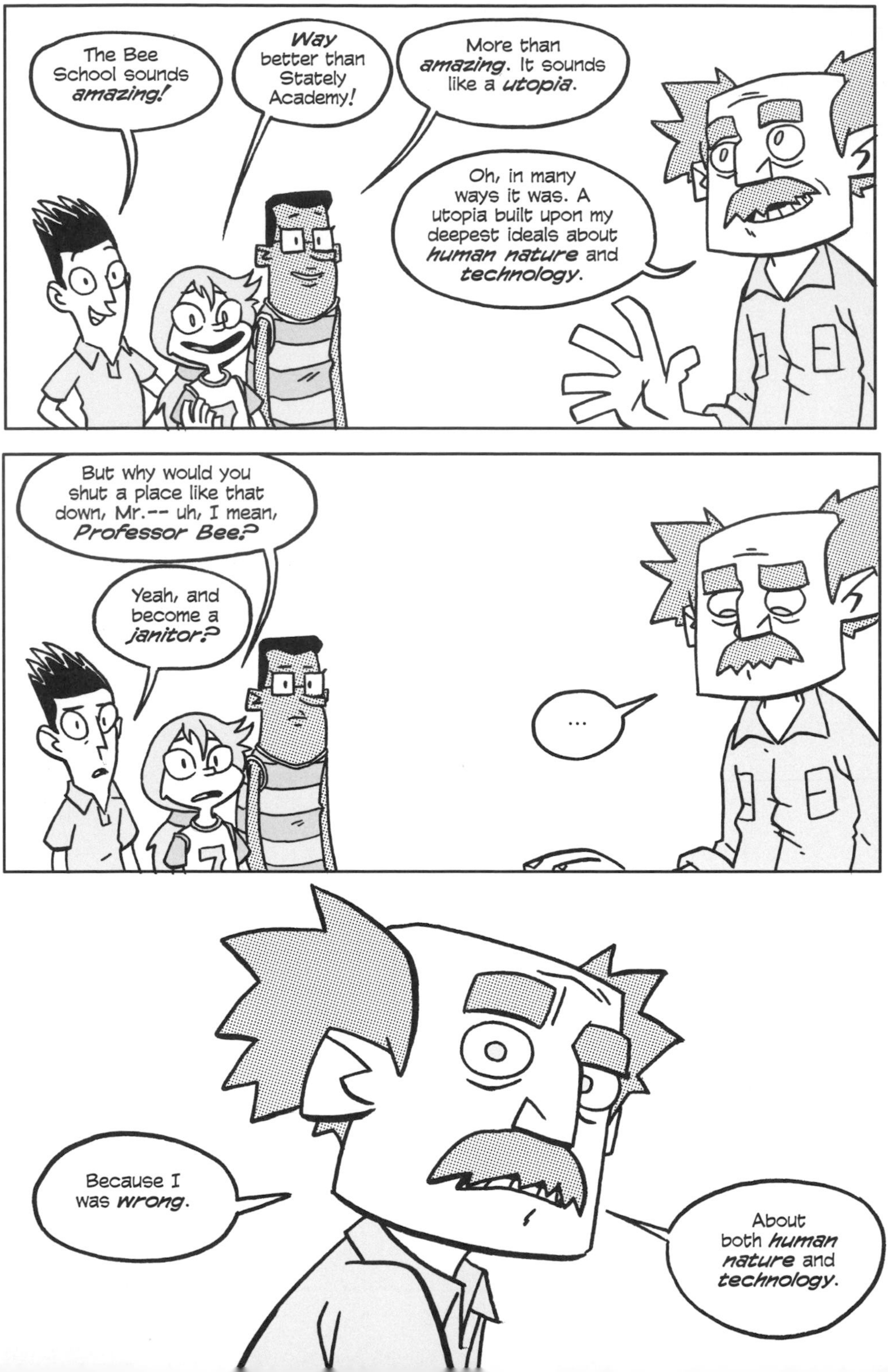
The Bee School sounds *amazing!*
Way better than Stately Academy!
More than *amazing*. It sounds like a *utopia*.
Oh, in many ways it was. A utopia built upon my deepest ideals about *human nature* and *technology*.
But why would you shut a place like that down, Mr.-- uh, I mean, *Professor Bee?*
Yeah, and become a *janitor?*
...
Because I was *wrong*.
About both *human nature* and *technology*.

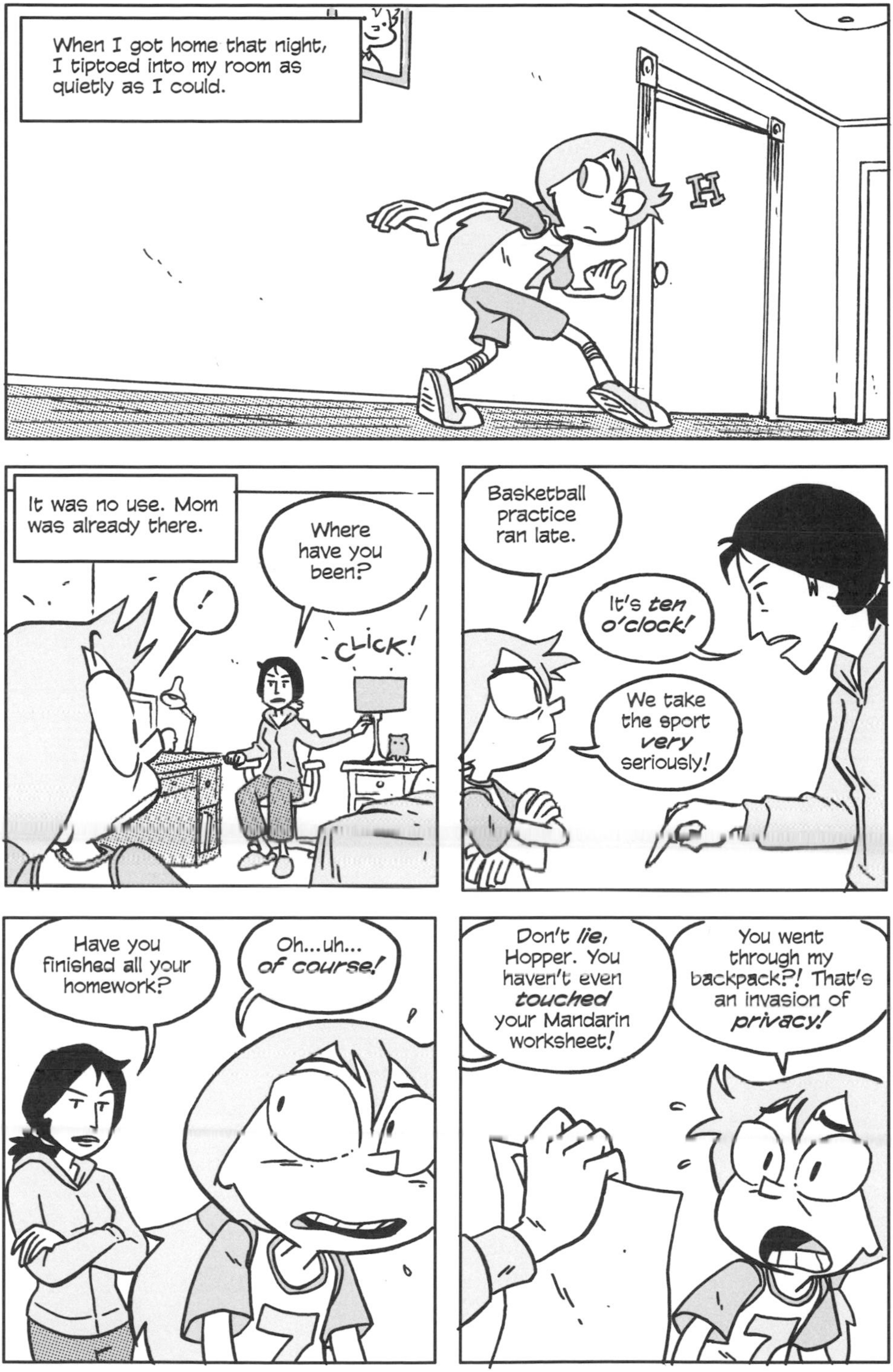
When I got home that night, I tiptoed into my room as quietly as I could.
It was no use. Mom was already there.
!
Where have you been?
CLICK!
Basketball practice ran late.
It's *ten o'clock!*
We take the sport *very* seriously!
Have you finished all your homework?
Oh...uh... *of course!*
Don't *lie*, Hopper. You haven't even *touched* your Mandarin worksheet!
You went through my backpack?! That's an invasion of *privacy!*

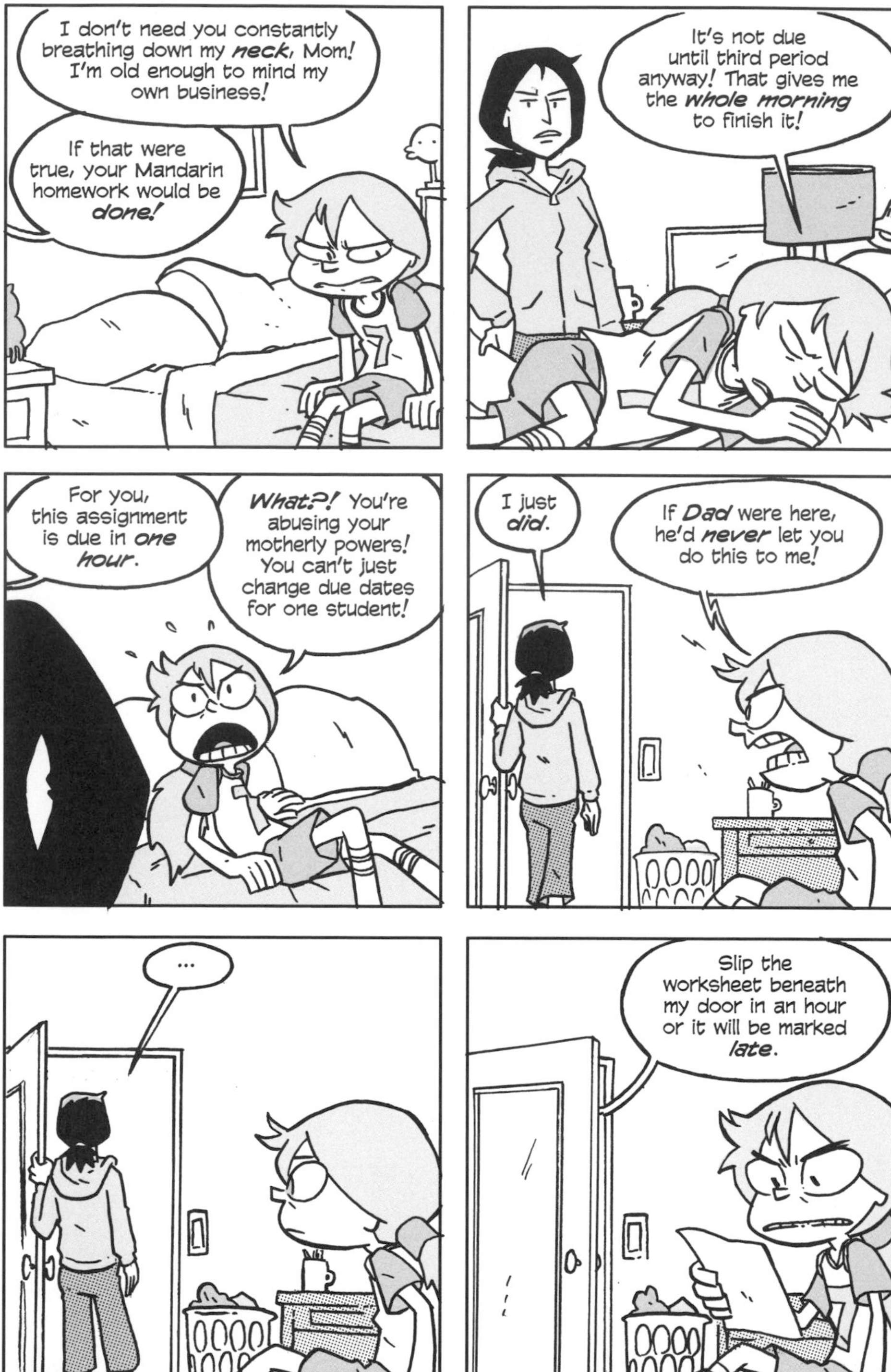
I don't need you constantly breathing down my *neck*, Mom! I'm old enough to mind my own business!
If that were true, your Mandarin homework would be *done!*
It's not due until third period anyway! That gives me the *whole morning* to finish it!
For you, this assignment is due in *one hour*.
What?! You're abusing your motherly powers! You can't just change due dates for one student!
I just *did*.
If *Dad* were here, he'd *never* let you do this to me!
...
Slip the worksheet beneath my door in an hour or it will be marked *late*.

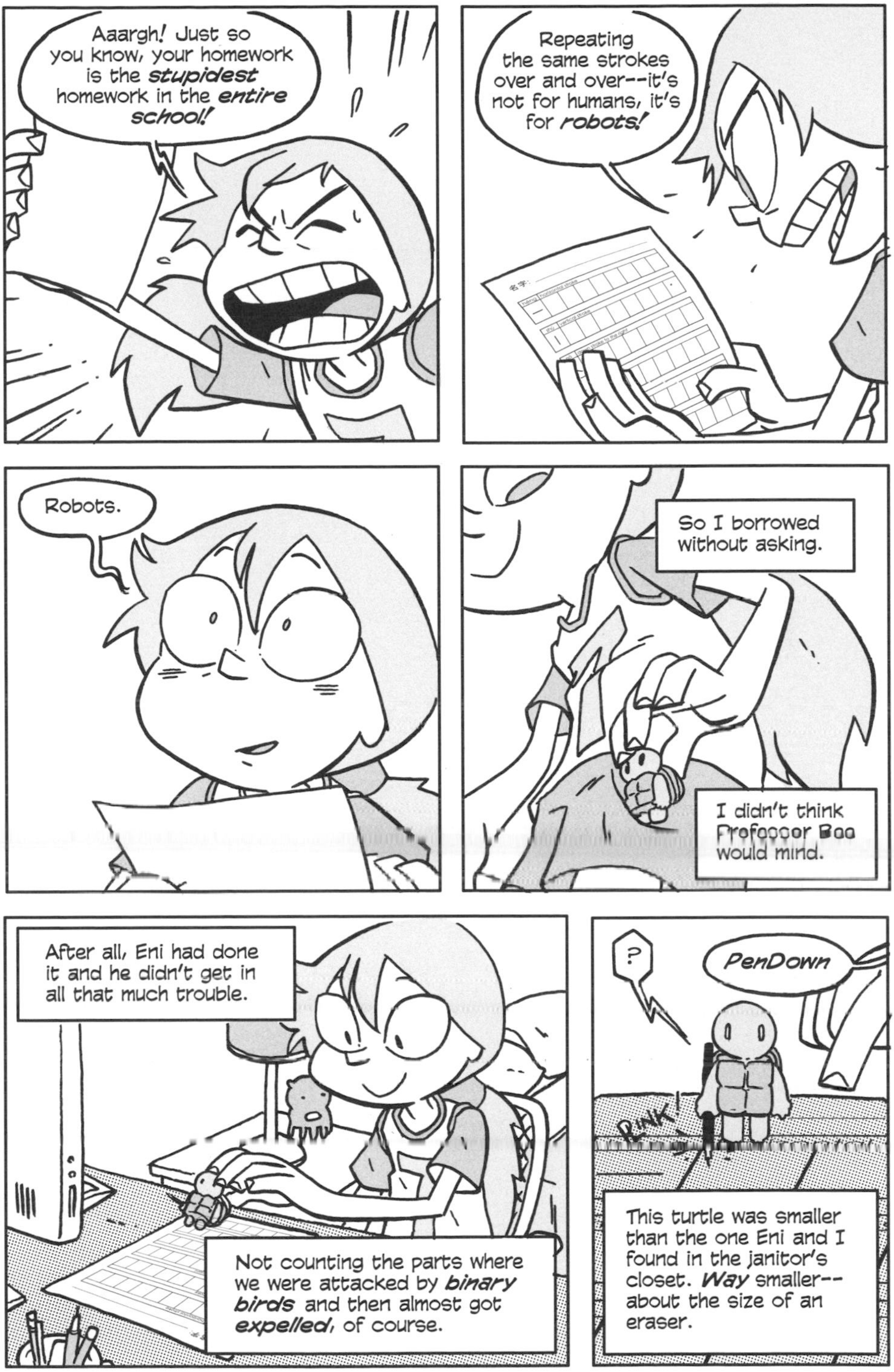

Aaargh! Just so you know, your homework is the ***stupidest*** homework in the ***entire school!***
Repeating the same strokes over and over--it's not for humans, it's for ***robots!***
Robots.
So I borrowed without asking.
I didn't think Professor Bee would mind.
After all, Eni had done it and he didn't get in all that much trouble.
Not counting the parts where we were attacked by ***binary birds*** and then almost got ***expelled***, of course.
?
PenDown
PINK!
This turtle was smaller than the one Eni and I found in the janitor's closet. ***Way*** smaller--about the size of an eraser.

It worked on a smaller scale, too, because its footsteps were smaller.

? Forward 12

héng horizontal stroke

Even though I was just starting out, my thinking had already changed. I could see patterns all around me.

The six rows on that worksheet were *six little programs* waiting to be coded.

héng | horizontal stroke ?

shù | vertical stroke

nà | down stroke to the right

tí | upward stroke

28

I closed my eyes and did the first one.

Repeat 7 [
  PenUp
  Forward 4
  PenDown
  Forward 12
]

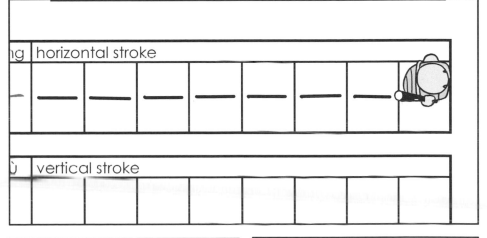

horizontal stroke

vertical stroke

Worked like a charm.

Yes!

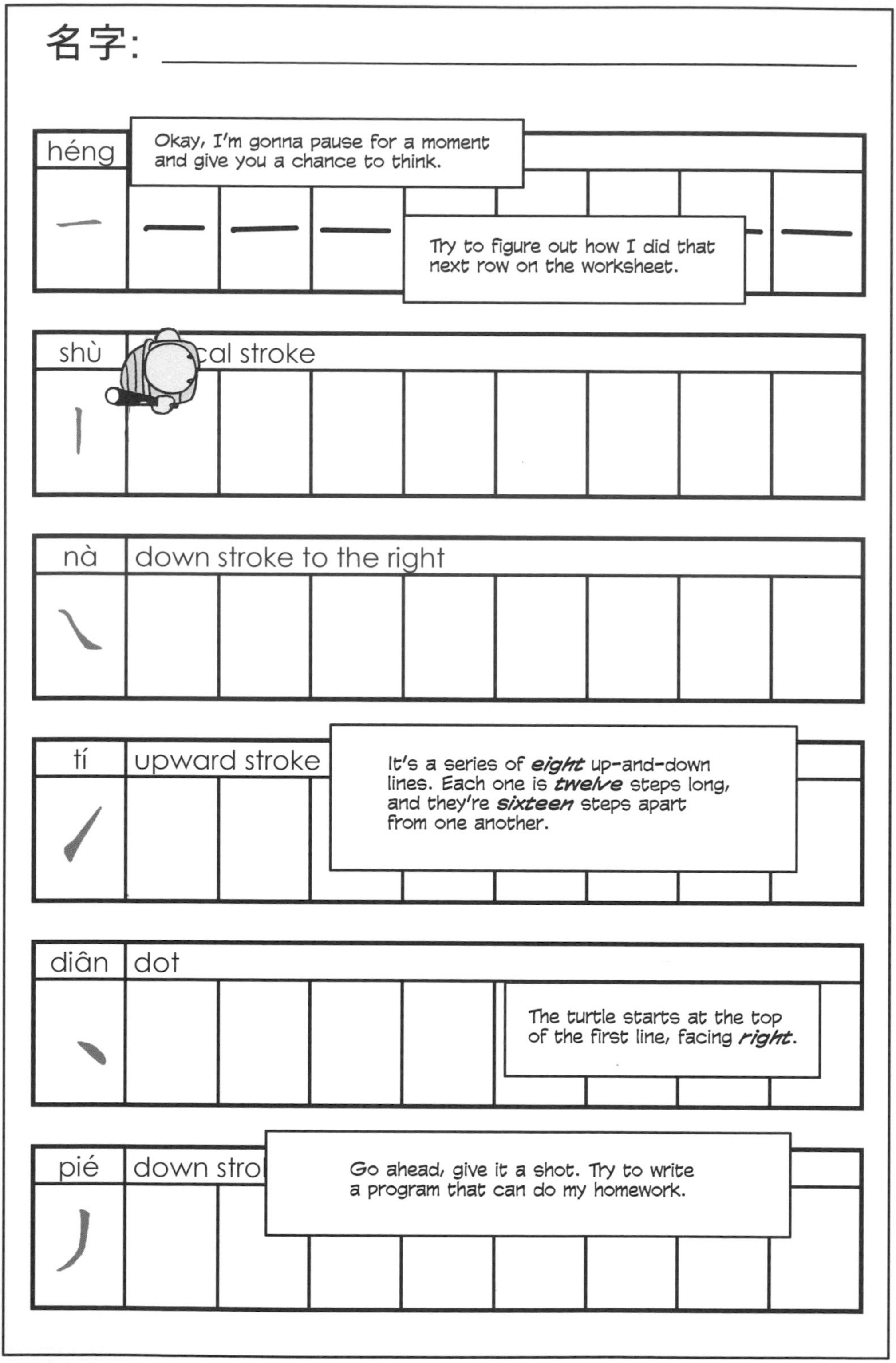

名字:
héng
Okay, I'm gonna pause for a moment and give you a chance to think.
Try to figure out how I did that next row on the worksheet.
shù
cal stroke
nà
down stroke to the right
tí
upward stroke
It's a series of ***eight*** up-and-down lines. Each one is ***twelve*** steps long, and they're ***sixteen*** steps apart from one another.
diân
dot
The turtle starts at the top of the first line, facing ***right***.
pié
down stro
Go ahead, give it a shot. Try to write a program that can do my homework.

Chapter

Compared to Professor Bee's Path Portals, the Mandarin worksheet wasn't all that bad.

shù vertical stroke

shù vertical stroke

shù vertical stroke

Turn right

--draw a line--

--and then get in position to draw the next line.

Repeat that *eight* times and we're done!

There are lots of different ways to draw those 8 lines. Here's how I did it:

```
Repeat 8 [
   Right 90
   PenDown
   Forward 12
   PenUp
   Left 90
   Forward 16
   Left 90
   Forward 12
   Right 90
]
```

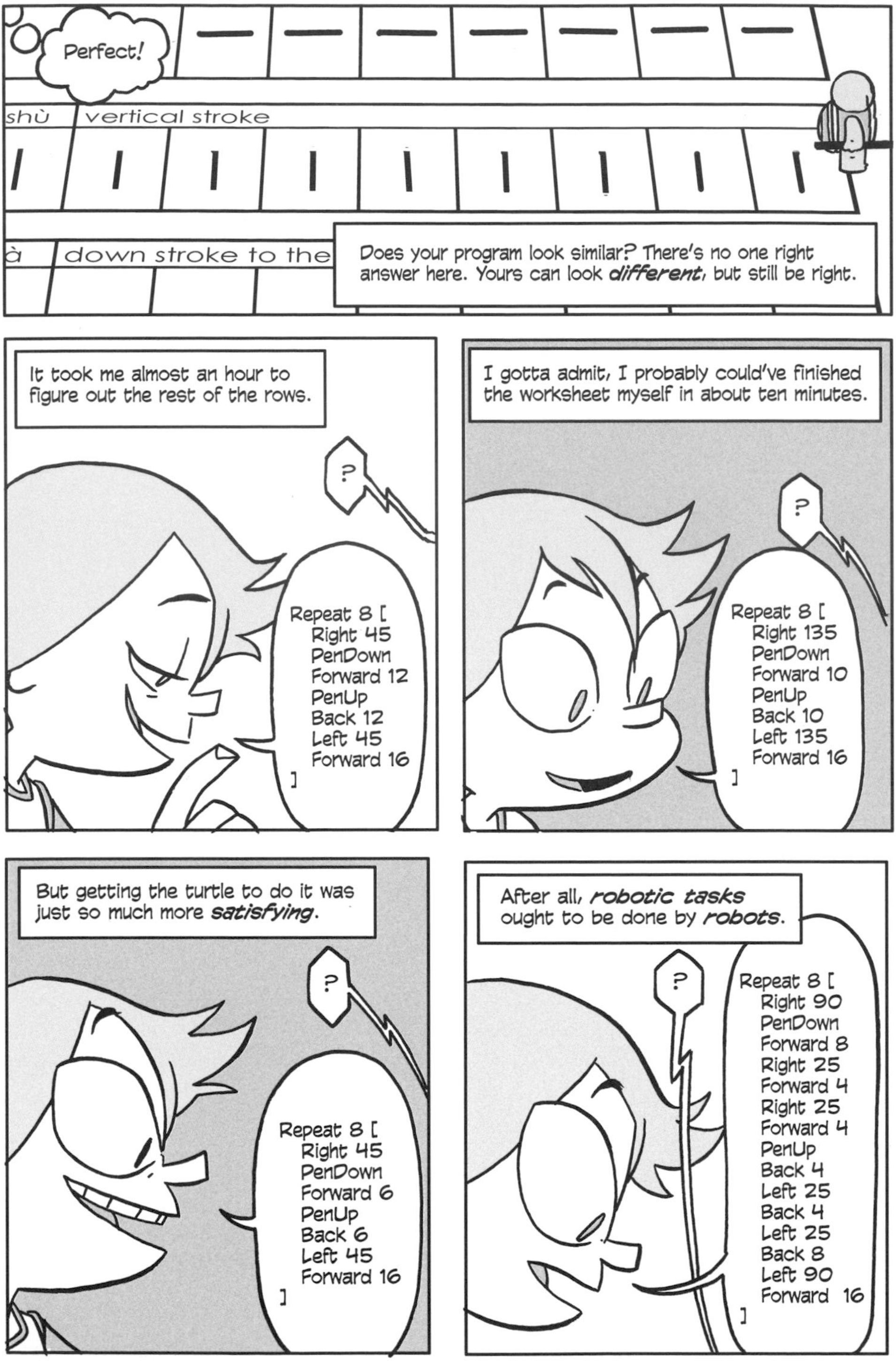
Perfect!
shù
vertical stroke
à
down stroke to the
Does your program look similar? There's no one right answer here. Yours can look *different*, but still be right.
It took me almost an hour to figure out the rest of the rows.
?
Repeat 8 [Right 45 PenDown Forward 12 PenUp Back 12 Left 45 Forward 16]
I gotta admit, I probably could've finished the worksheet myself in about ten minutes.
?
Repeat 8 [Right 135 PenDown Forward 10 PenUp Back 10 Left 135 Forward 16]
But getting the turtle to do it was just so much more *satisfying*.
?
Repeat 8 [Right 45 PenDown Forward 6 PenUp Back 6 Left 45 Forward 16]
After all, *robotic tasks* ought to be done by *robots*.
?
Repeat 8 [Right 90 PenDown Forward 8 Right 25 Forward 4 Right 25 Forward 4 PenUp Back 4 Left 25 Back 4 Left 25 Back 8 Left 90 Forward 16]

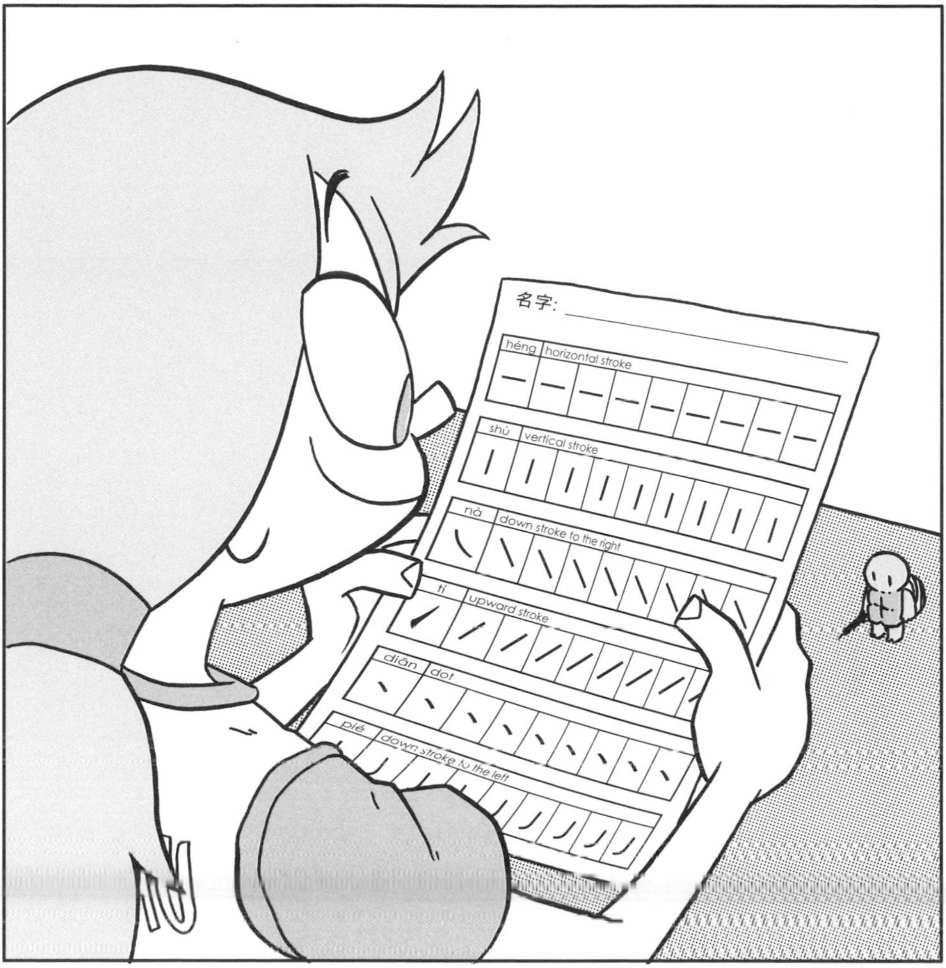
名字:
héng horizontal stroke
shù vertical stroke
nà down stroke to the right
tí upward stroke
diân dot
pié down stroke to the left

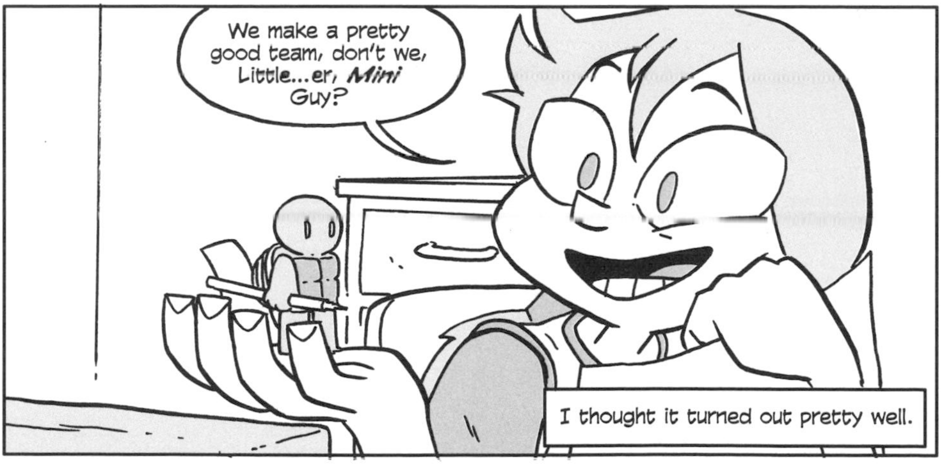
We make a pretty good team, don't we, Little...er, *Mini* Guy?
I thought it turned out pretty well.

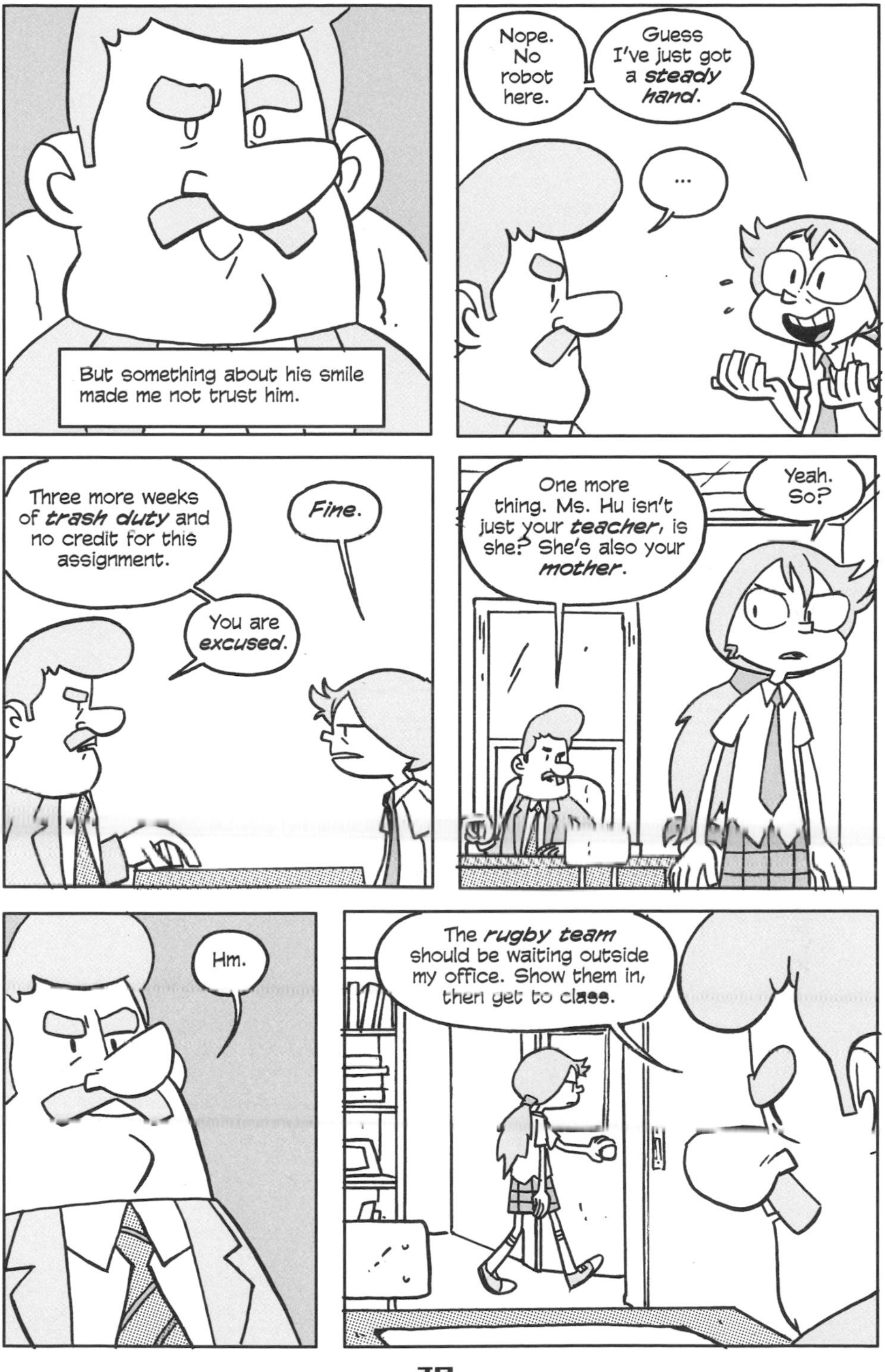
But something about his smile made me not trust him.
Nope. No robot here.
Guess I've just got a *steady hand*.
...
Three more weeks of *trash duty* and no credit for this assignment.
You are *excused*.
Fine.
One more thing. Ms. Hu isn't just your *teacher*, is she? She's also your *mother*.
Yeah. So?
Hm.
The *rugby team* should be waiting outside my office. Show them in, then get to class.

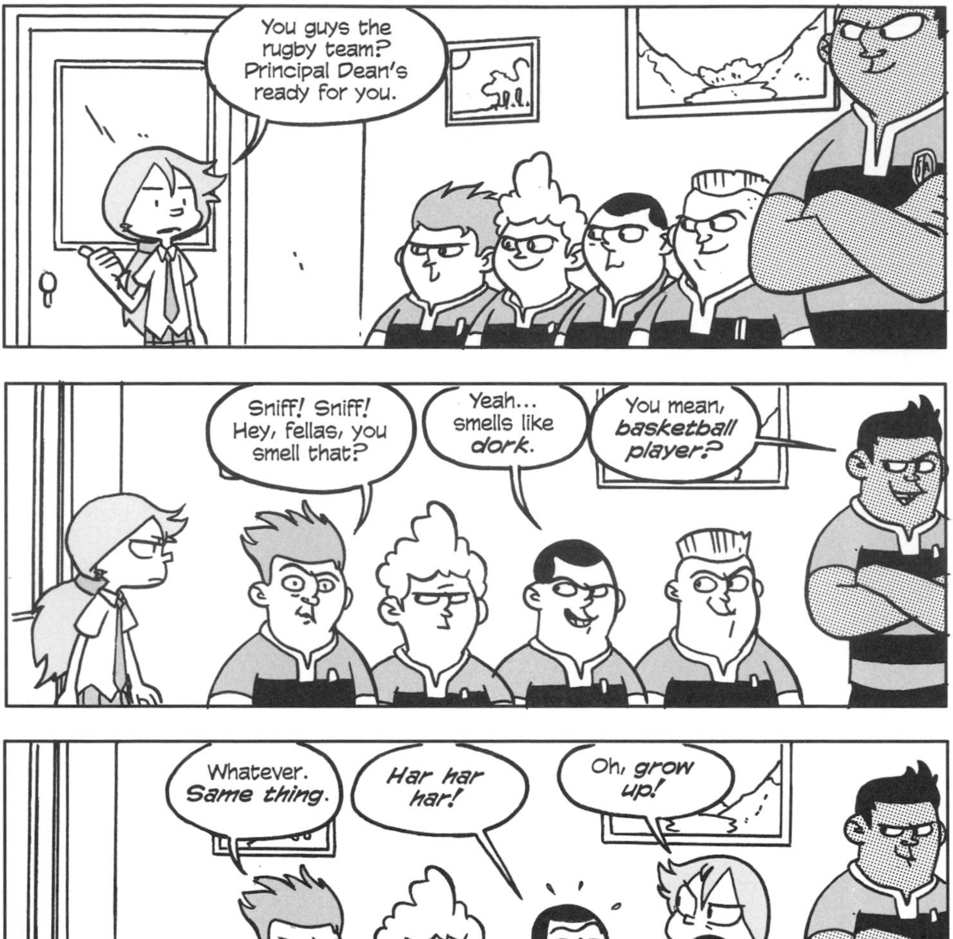
You guys the rugby team? Principal Dean's ready for you.
Sniff! Sniff! Hey, fellas, you smell that?
Yeah... smells like *dork*.
You mean, ***basketball player?***
Whatever. ***Same thing.***
Har har har!
Oh, ***grow up!***
Sorry to break it to you, Dork Girl, but if there's no ***tackling***, it's not a ***real sport!***

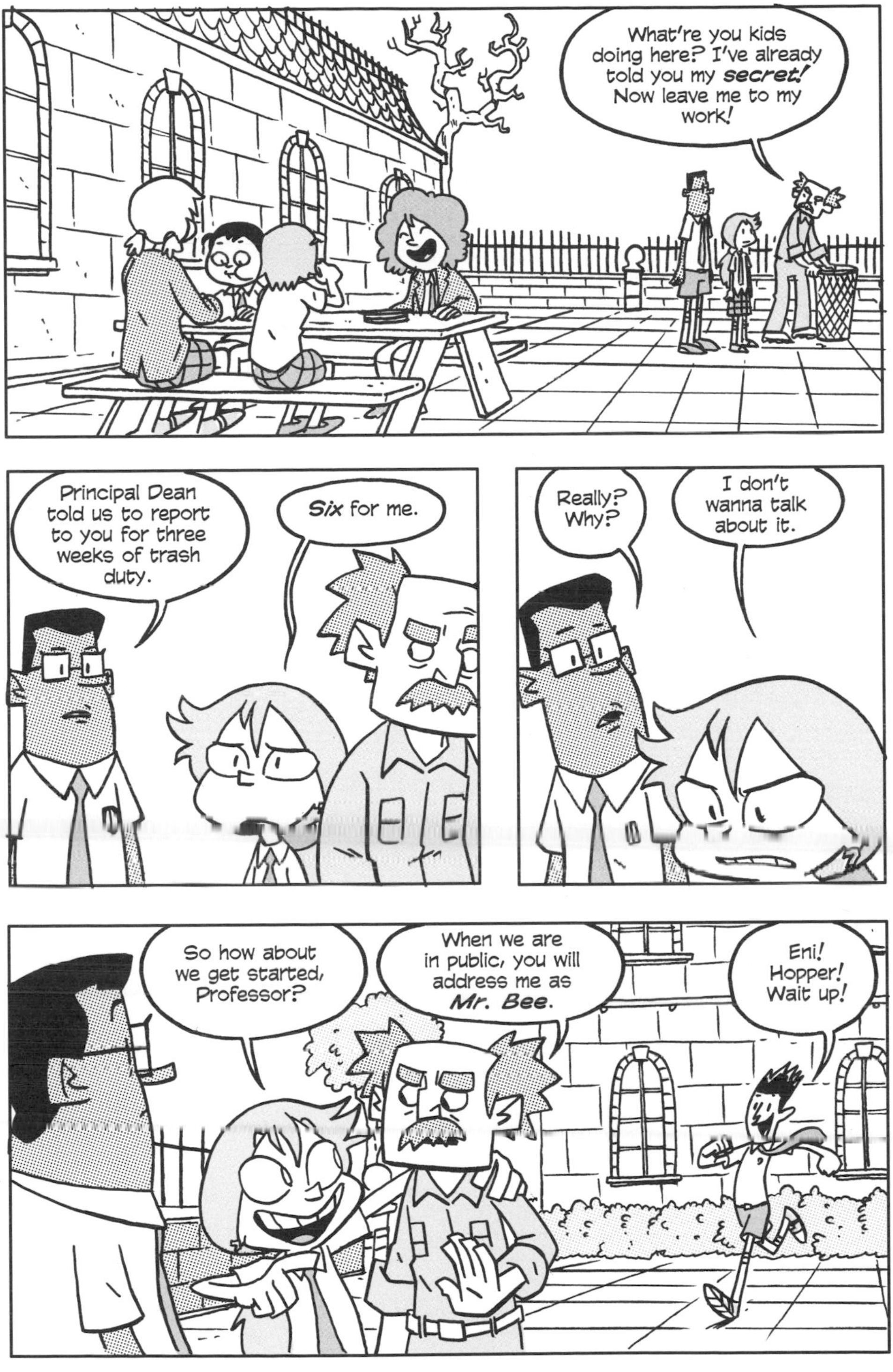
What're you kids doing here? I've already told you my *secret!* Now leave me to my work!
Principal Dean told us to report to you for three weeks of trash duty.
Six for me.
Really? Why?
I don't wanna talk about it.
So how about we get started, Professor?
When we are in public, you will address me as *Mr. Bee*.
Eni! Hopper! Wait up!

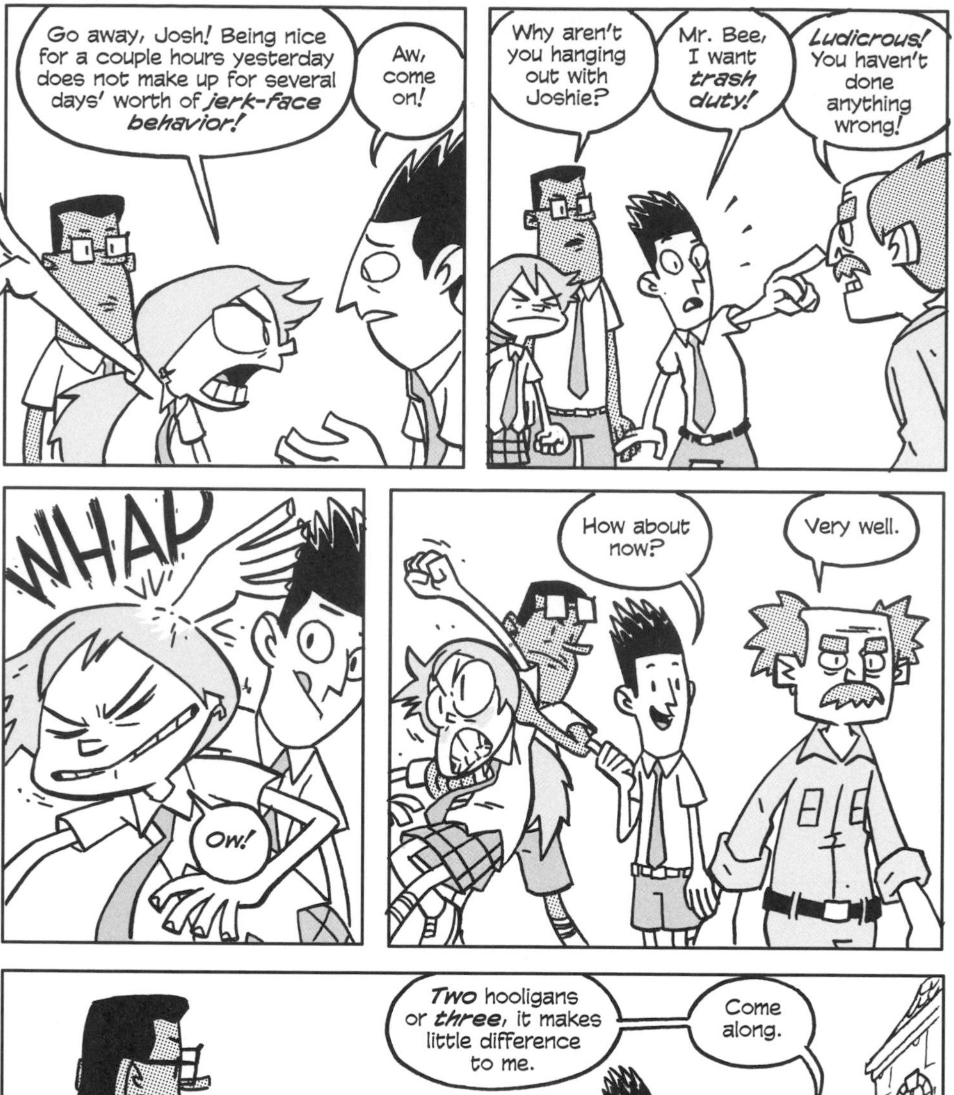
Go away, Josh! Being nice for a couple hours yesterday does not make up for several days' worth of *jerk-face behavior!*
Aw, come on!
Why aren't you hanging out with Joshie?
Mr. Bee, I want *trash duty!*
Ludicrous! You haven't done anything wrong!
WHAP
Ow!
How about now?
Very well.
Two hooligans or *three*, it makes little difference to me.
Come along.

41

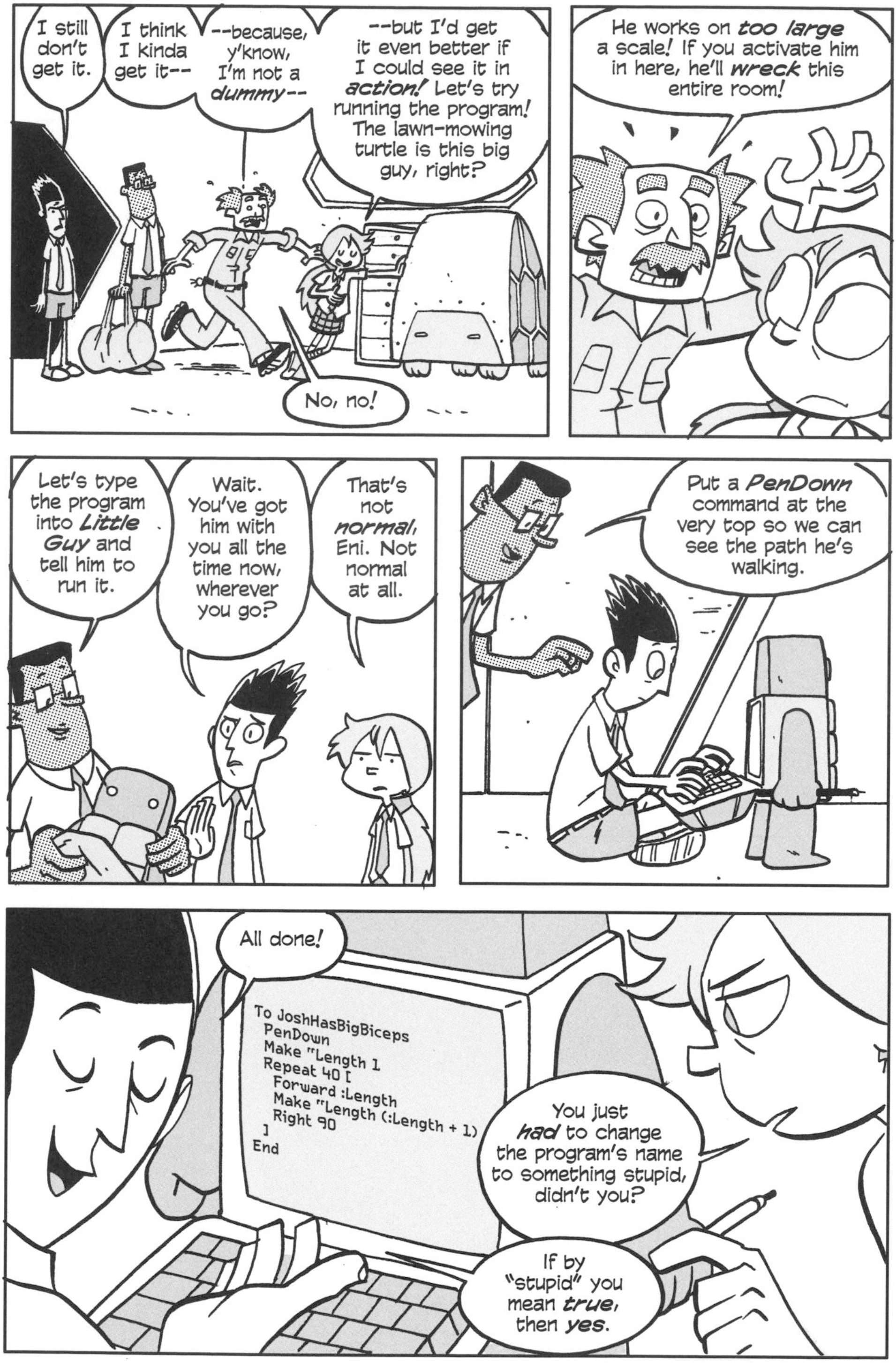

I still don't get it.
I think I kinda get it--
--because, y'know, I'm not a *dummy*--
--but I'd get it even better if I could see it in *action!* Let's try running the program! The lawn-mowing turtle is this big guy, right?
No, no!
He works on *too large* a scale! If you activate him in here, he'll *wreck* this entire room!
Let's type the program into *Little Guy* and tell him to run it.
Wait. You've got him with you all the time now, wherever you go?
That's not *normal*, Eni. Not normal at all.
Put a *PenDown* command at the very top so we can see the path he's walking.
All done!
To JoshHasBigBiceps
PenDown
Make "Length 1
Repeat 40 [
Forward :Length
Make "Length (:Length + 1)
Right 90
]
End
You just *had* to change the program's name to something stupid, didn't you?
If by "stupid" you mean *true*, then *yes*.

Panel 1 (speech bubble): JoshHasBigBiceps

Panel 2 (narration box): To keep myself from decking Josh, I focused on what the turtle was doing.

Panel 3 (code):
```
To JoshHasBigBiceps
 PenDown
 Make "Length 1
 Repeat 40 [
  Forward :Length
  Make "Length (:Length + 1)
  Right 90
 ]
End
```

LENGTH 1

Panel 4 (speech bubble): All right, Little Guy, you're gonna repeat the next three lines *forty* times!

```
To JoshHasBigBiceps
 PenDown
 Make "Length 1
 Repeat 40 [
  Forward :Length
  Make "Length (:Length + 1)
  Right 90
 ]
End
```

LENGTH 1

Panel 5 (code):
```
To JoshHasBigBiceps
 PenDown
 Make "Length 1
 Repeat 40 [
  Forward :Length
  Make "Length (:Length + 1)
  Right 90
 ]
End
```

LENGTH 2

45

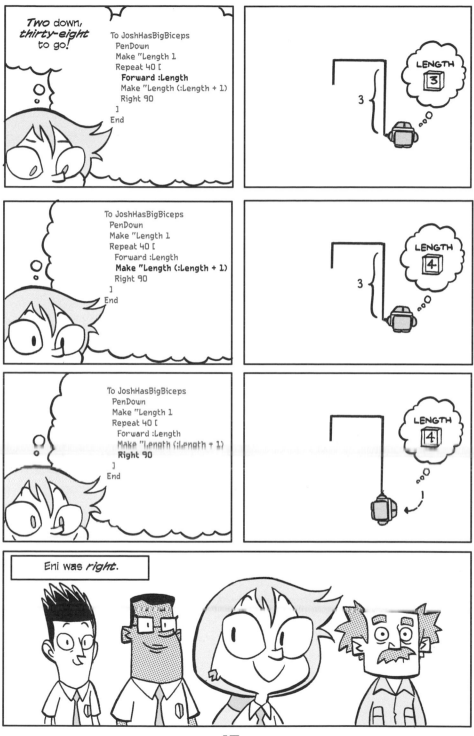

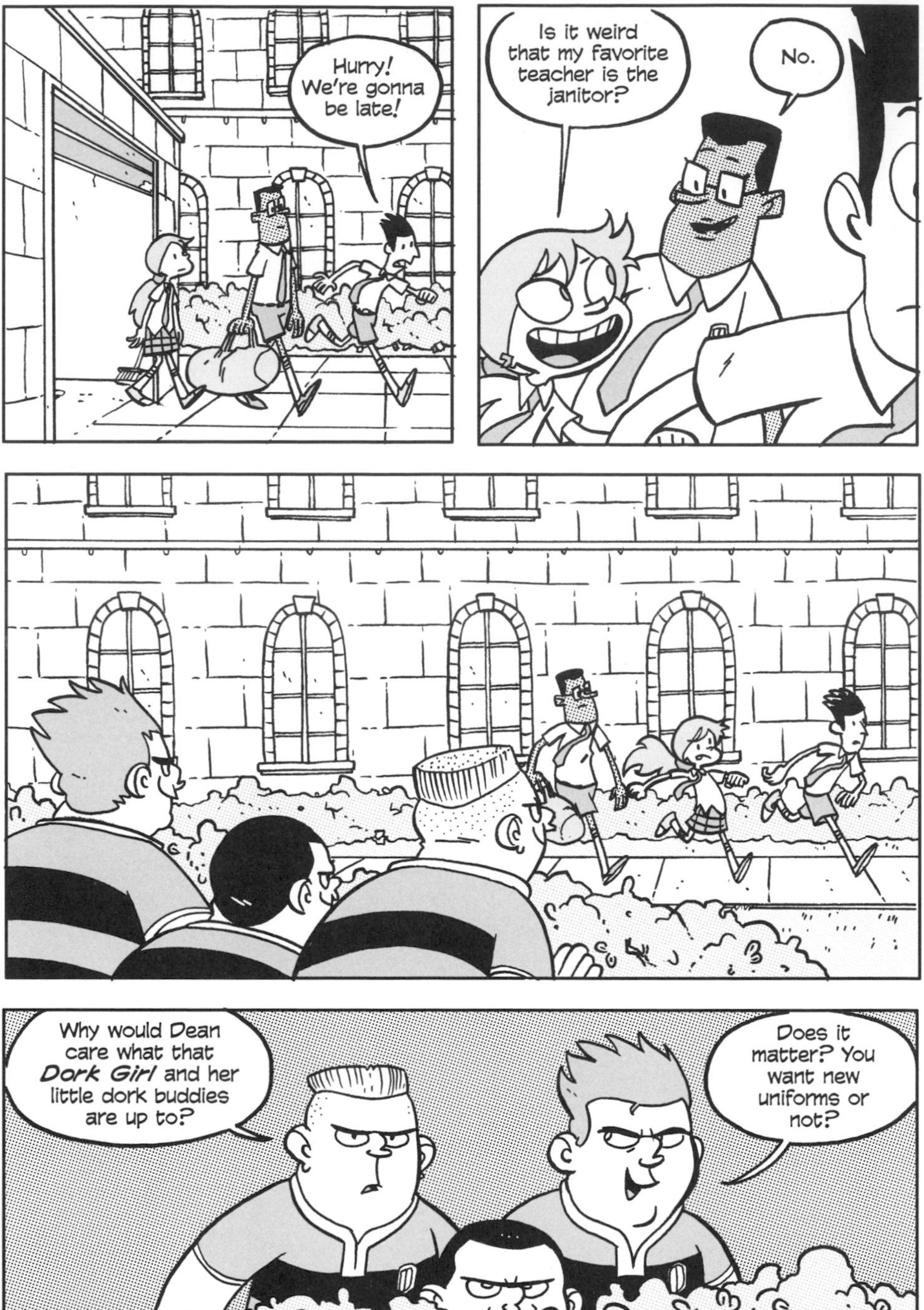

Hurry! We're gonna be late!
Is it weird that my favorite teacher is the janitor?
No.
Why would Dean care what that *Dork Girl* and her little dork buddies are up to?
Does it matter? You want new uniforms or not?

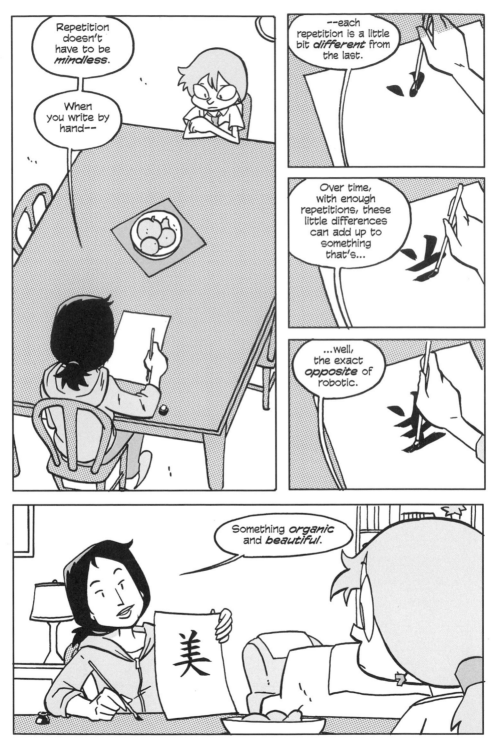

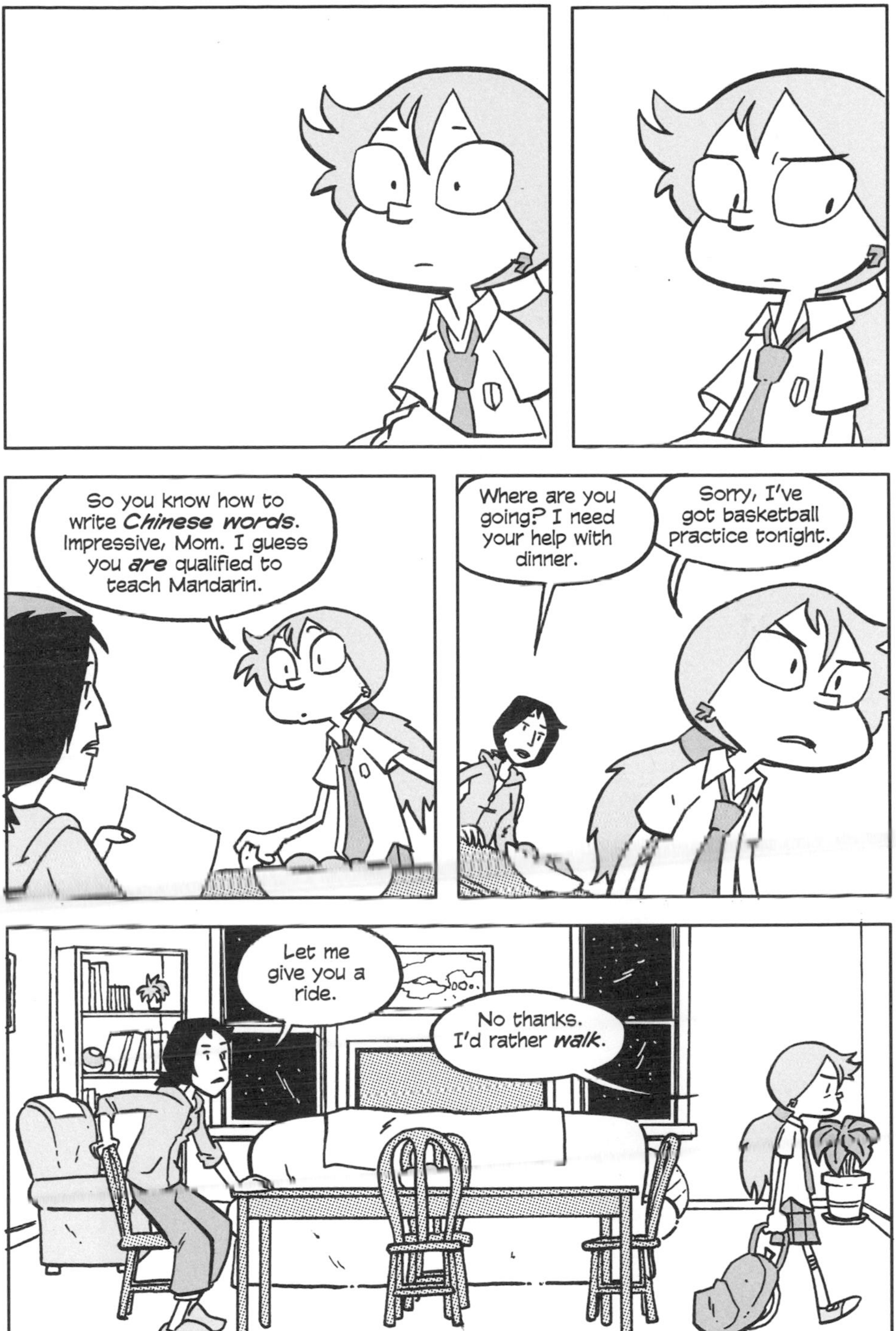
So you know how to write *Chinese words*. Impressive, Mom. I guess you *are* qualified to teach Mandarin.
Where are you going? I need your help with dinner.
Sorry, I've got basketball practice tonight.
Let me give you a ride.
No thanks. I'd rather *walk*.

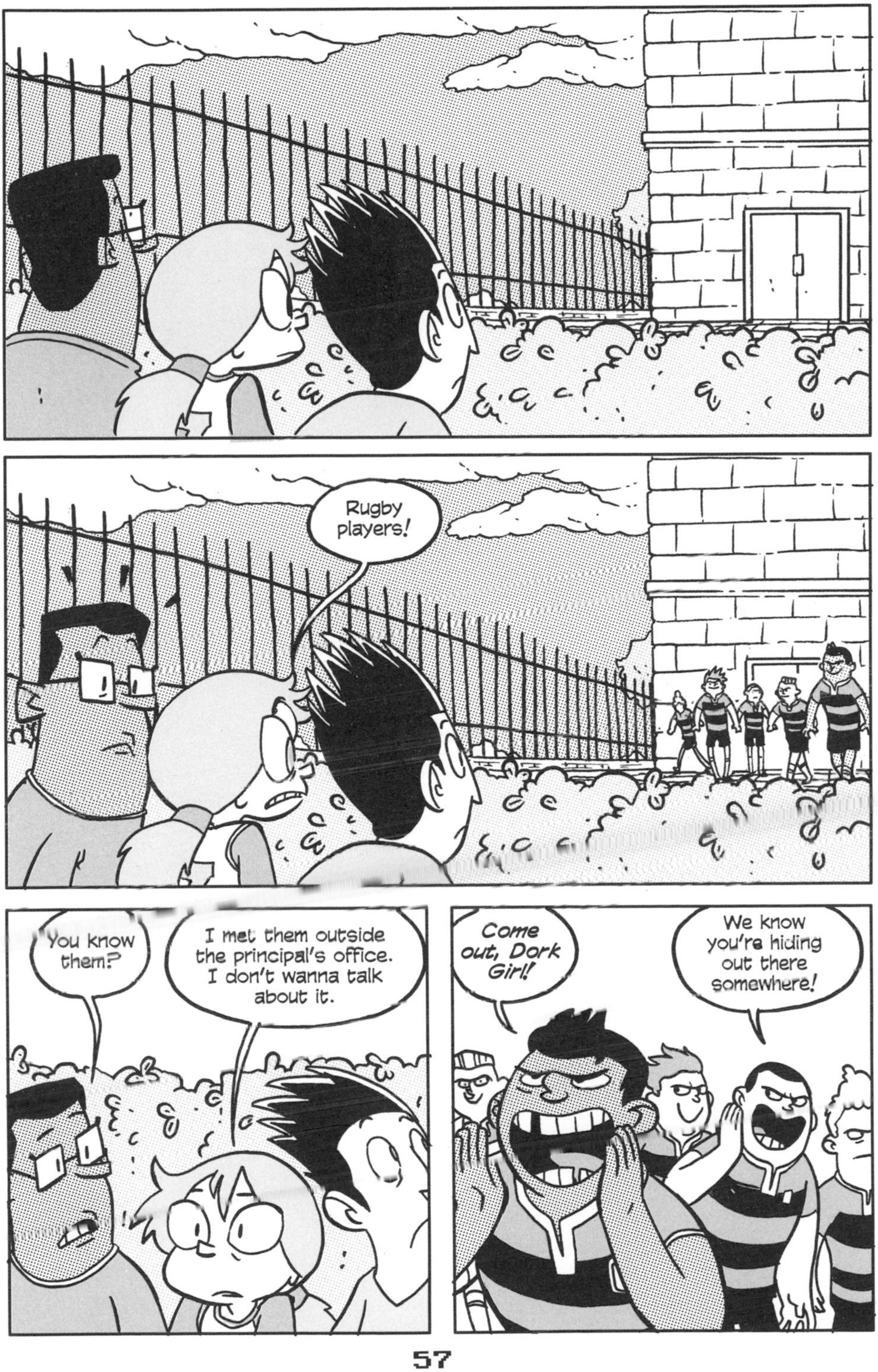
Rugby players!
You know them?
I met them outside the principal's office. I don't wanna talk about it.
Come out, Dork Girl!
We know you're hiding out there somewhere!

Chapter

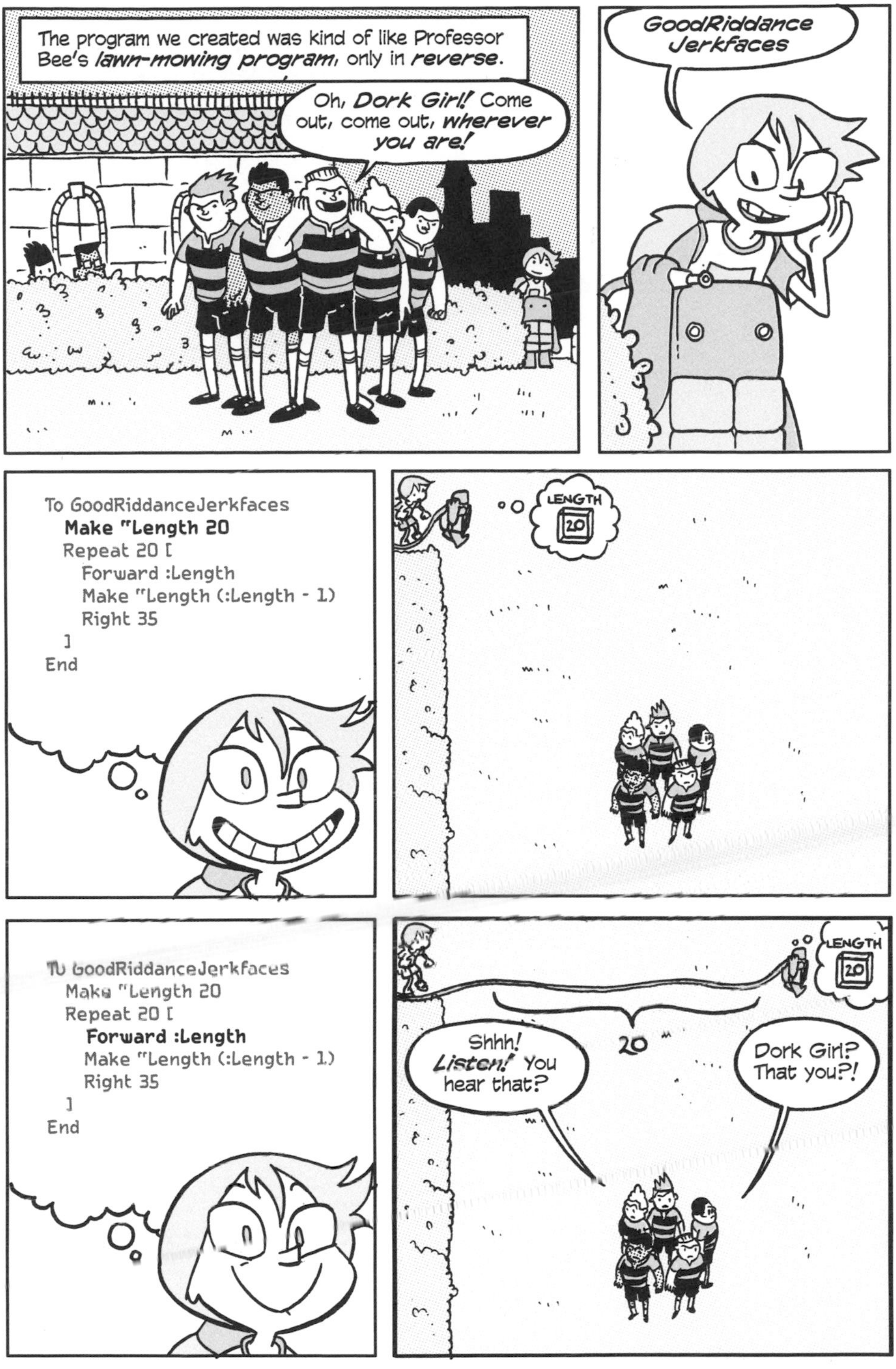

The program we created was kind of like Professor Bee's *lawn-mowing program*, only in *reverse*.
Oh, ***Dork Girl!*** Come out, come out, ***wherever you are!***
GoodRiddance Jerkfaces
To GoodRiddanceJerkfaces
Make "Length 20
Repeat 20 [
Forward :Length
Make "Length (:Length - 1)
Right 35
]
End
LENGTH
20
To GoodRiddanceJerkfaces
Make "Length 20
Repeat 20 [
Forward :Length
Make "Length (:Length - 1)
Right 35
]
End
LENGTH
20
20
Shhh! ***Listen!*** You hear that?
Dork Girl? That you?!

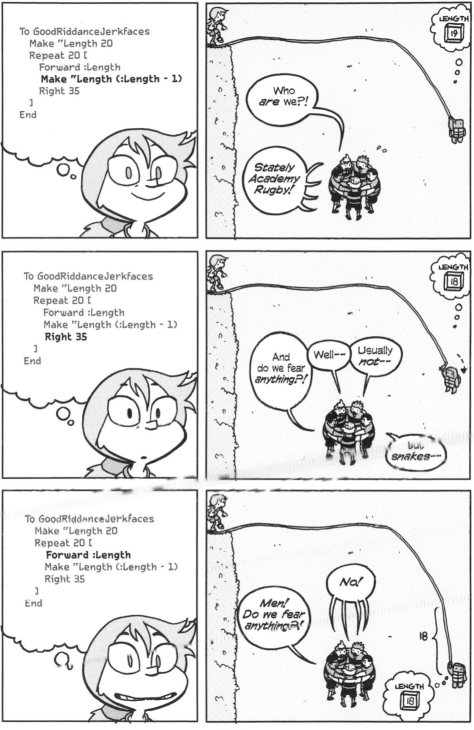

73

85

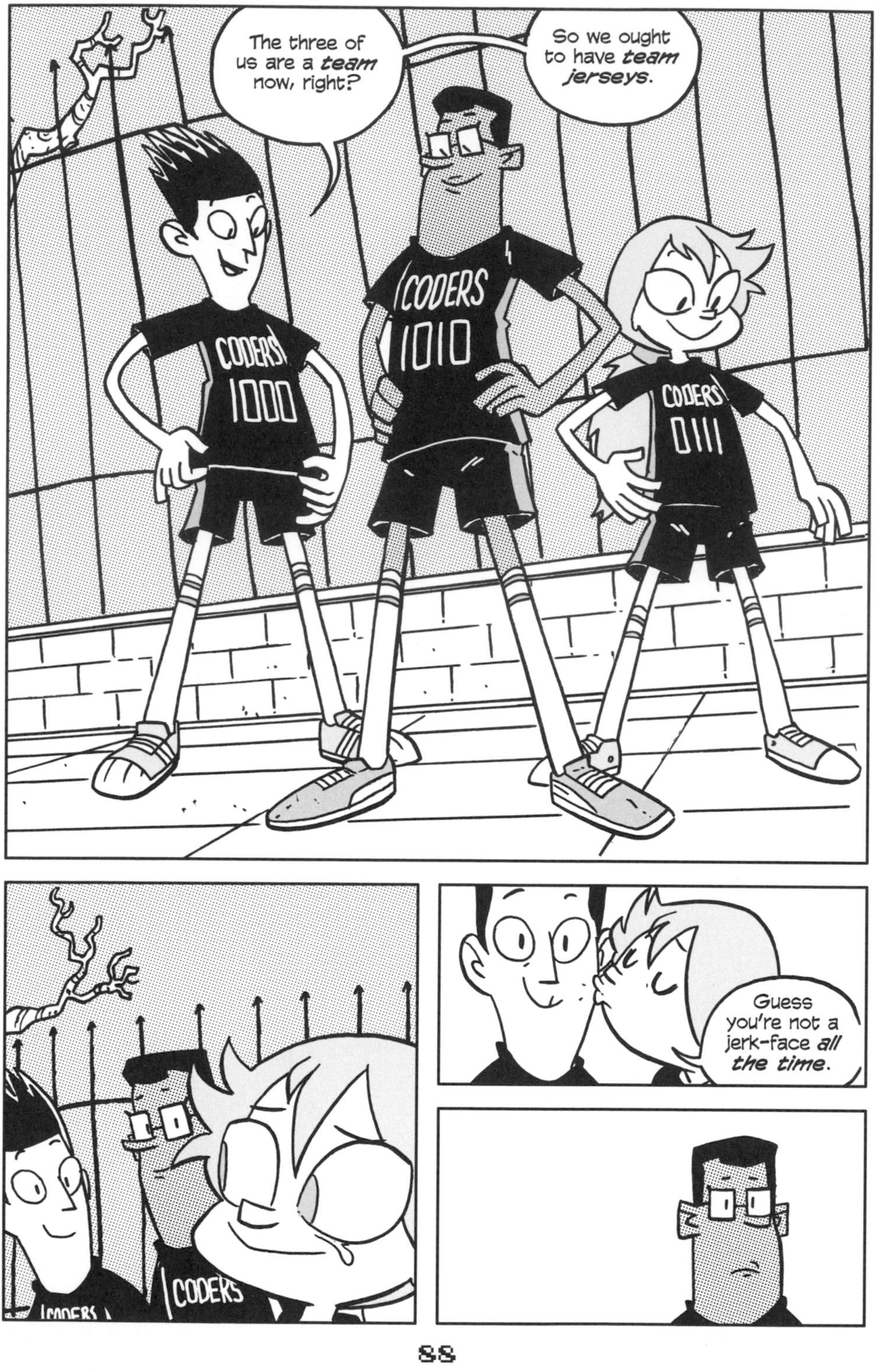
The three of us are a ***team*** now, right?
So we ought to have ***team jerseys***.
CODERS 1000
CODERS 1010
CODERS 0111
CODERS
Guess you're not a jerk-face ***all the time***.

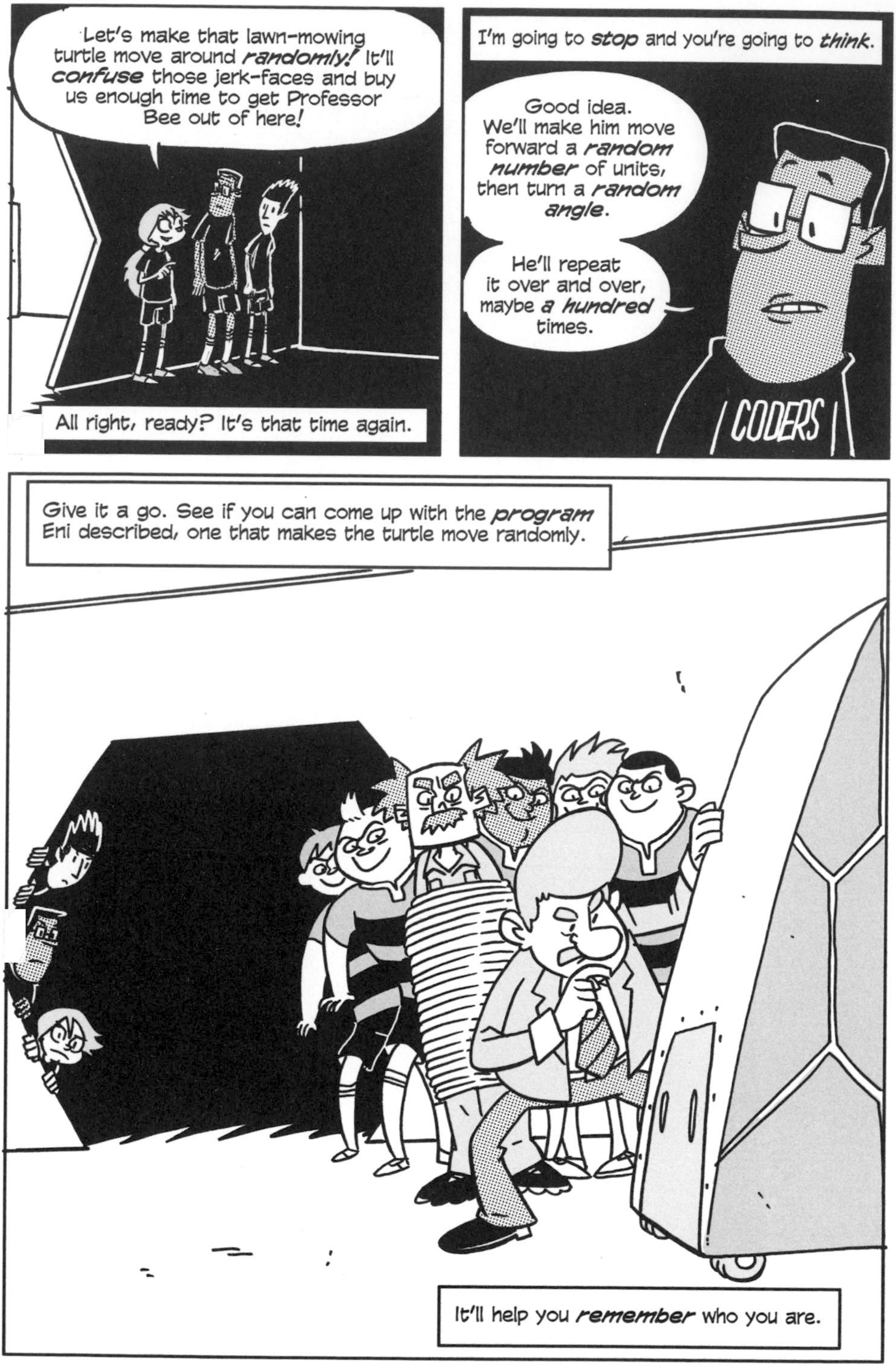
Let's make that lawn-mowing turtle move around *randomly!* It'll *confuse* those jerk-faces and buy us enough time to get Professor Bee out of here!
All right, ready? It's that time again.
I'm going to *stop* and you're going to *think*.
Good idea. We'll make him move forward a *random number* of units, then turn a *random angle*.
He'll repeat it over and over, maybe *a hundred* times.
CODERS
Give it a go. See if you can come up with the *program* Eni described, one that makes the turtle move randomly.
It'll help you *remember* who you are.

Continued in

Secrets & Sequences

Ready to start coding?

Visit www.secret-coders.com